Praise for *Mr Geography*

'*Mr Geography* is the work of a writer operating at the height of his powers. One follows the twists and turns of this story of discovery and self-discovery in a sustained state of delight' **J. M. Coetzee**, Booker Prize-winning author of *Disgrace*

'Tim Parks tells of a trek across Switzerland and into the past of his protagonist, each journey as eventful and adventurous as the other. *Mr Geography* is a beguiling tale about love and betrayal, wrong turns, dangerous aberrations and late salvation' **Peter Stamm**, author of *Seven Years*

'Journeys and quests are the stock in trade of novels; but this one shines thanks to its brilliant layering of time and place. It's impossible to guess where it will lead – and yet astonishing and hugely satisfying at the end' **Jane Rogers**, author of *Conrad and Eleanor*

'A quicksilvery syntax slips through this compelling story of desire and loss and what it is to be a lonely man – so that each page, each paragraph, even, shifts between time zones and circumstances to give us a novel that keeps us at the very edge of our attention' **Kirsty Gunn**, author of *The Big Music*

'For forty years, Tim Parks has written, with accelerating acuity, about Italy, Europe, literature, art and above all the body – the body in relation to art. What survives? What doesn't? If everything goes away, as it does, what is worth doing? What isn't? *Mr Geography* is the fullest and most powerful expression yet of Parks's (and "our") obsessive concerns and themes' **David Shields**, author of *The Thing About Life Is That One Day You'll Be Dead*

'Parks aficionados will recognise themes from his greatest works, *Goodness*, *Destiny* and *Sex is Forbidden*, but they will rejoice at the unsentimental tenderness, kindness and grace that he adds to the mix in this exquisite novel. Parks novices will simply wonder: where has this writer been all my life?' **Jan Wilm**

'An extraordinarily powerful, mo⁻ ˙
beautifully written and superb
author of *My Cri*

TIM PARKS

Mr Geography

Harvill
Secker

3 5 7 9 10 8 6 4

Harvill Secker, an imprint of Vintage, is part of the Penguin Random House group of companies whose addresses can be found at global.penguinrandomhouse.com

First published by Harvill Secker in 2024

penguin.co.uk/vintage

Typeset in 11.4/16.25pt Palatino LT Pro by Jouve (UK), Milton Keynes

Printed and bound in Great Britain by Clays Ltd, Elcograf S.p.A.

The authorised representative in the EEA is Penguin Random House Ireland, Morrison Chambers, 32 Nassau Street, Dublin D02 YH68

A CIP catalogue record for this book is available from the British Library

ISBN 9781787304536

Penguin Random House is committed to a sustainable future for our business, our readers and our planet. This book is made from Forest Stewardship Council® certified paper.

The kingdom of the world had no significance: what
could one do but wander about?

D. H. Lawrence, *Twilight in Italy*

Nothing like the mountains for remembering.

Paolo Cognetti, *The Eight Mountains*

'Lady Chatterleys Liebhaber'

Many years have passed, Julia is dead, and this summer I decided to complete the walk we only began. I flew to Zürich, took the train to Konstanz. I remembered Julia hadn't wanted to fly. She wanted to travel by boat and train, as Lawrence had done. So why didn't we? I can't recall. Perhaps it seemed important to get away fast. Or flights were cheaper.

I have booked a room at the Hotel Alte Post; the name rang a bell. It was here we stayed, I thought. But no, this is a modern, antiseptic, anonymous establishment. We had been in a shabby old place, with wood panelling and squeaky bedsprings. Unless there has been a radical make-over? It hardly matters. We punished the bedsprings and laughed. In our hearts, perhaps, we were afraid.

The present Alte Post is more comfortable. There are illustrations of airships on the walls. Stretching out for a few minutes, it occurs to me that this is actually my third time in the German–Swiss borderlands. I had come here between school and university, long ago, to work as a farmhand, near Basel. On that occasion I did travel by train. I remember reaching through the dark to touch the hand of the girl in the couchette opposite. We had been talking since Paris. I remember nothing of her physically. Nothing of what we spoke about. Not even her nationality. Only that it was my right hand I reached across the compartment; she let me hold hers; our heads were towards the window and a dimly lit platform where the train had stopped for a while. Then with a soft squeal the carriage began to roll and our fingers slid apart.

Konstanz seems entirely at ease with its blend of kitsch and quaint, its stone courtyards and half-timbered houses. Geraniums and tea rooms. How far is it important – I remember framing this question once for a mock A-level exam – that a tourist destination confirm its visitors' stereotypes? To reach the lakefront you follow the road under the railway lines; the low sunshine is sharp and the great expanse of water shimmers: the German shore, the Swiss, the Austrian. A paddle steamer thrashes towards the pier. Our opportunist present embalms the picturesque past; that might be a good answer. Flower beds along the shore are laid out with impeccable symmetry, trees pruned to neat umbrellas of shade. On the steamer people are pressing at the rails. A sailor loops his rope over a piling and pulls it tight.

Back in the centre we had shaken our heads over the price of rings. There are so many jewellers in Konstanz. Not yet, Julia sighed. This evening I stand in front of a window displaying a watch on a gnarled log, as if it were some kind of shiny fungus. The hands point to 8.25. €2,700 the tag says. Time, I think, for me to find a table and order beer and salad with sausage. €26. Eating, I study the map on my phone: the river flows west out of the lake, towards Schaffhausen and Rhine Falls. The first boat leaves at 9.12 a.m.

Können wir uns dazusetzen?

It's a young couple with a crying child; the table has benches both sides. *Natürlich*, I nod. You didn't tell me you knew German, Julia had accused. She was delighted. She mussed my hair. That will make things easier! Only a few words, I protested. *Schweizerdeutsch*. So many things, she said, we still don't know about each other.

The mother picks up the toddler and paces back and forth. They're waiting for their food.

Ferien? the man asks.

Kind of.

He switches to English, a handsome young professional with a neatly trimmed moustache. Earring. Tattoo.

You are travelling?

Yes.

To where?

I have no desire to explain. But nor to be impolite. They seem nice people.

Across Switzerland.

You must go to Winterthur – the mother comes back to say – where we live. The little boy is clutching a frog that squeaks as he opens and closes his hand. There is a fine Kunstmuseum. Picasso. Caspar David Friedrich. Bruegel.

I'm sure he has plans already, the man smiles. Evidently it's a pleasure for these two to use their English, which is excellent. I notice now that the tattoo, on the pale flesh inside the man's forearm, shows an old-fashioned compass. North is his elbow. At other tables all around the customers seem cheerful and relaxed.

I try to calm myself. Wearing a loose dress, the mother exudes a sort of flustered sensuality. The little boy is the spitting image of his father. Julia agreed that children were out of the question. Across the table, the young father lifts an enquiring eyebrow.

I am following a route, I offer, that an English writer walked, in 1913, from Konstanz to Como, in Italy.

But that is a long way!

The waitress sets down plates of pork. The boy is refusing to be strapped to his seat.

Which writer?

D. H. Lawrence. *Zahlen, bitte?* I catch the waitress.

Lady Chatterleys Liebhaber! the mother remembers.

You are a professor, the man asks. Of literature?

I'm on my feet now. Not at all, I bow, just a whim. *Guten Appetit.*

'When I went from Constance . . .'

The boat is not going to Schaffhausen, sir.

My plans are foiled before I start.

Only Stein am Rhein. This . . . *Trockenheit*. The water is too flat.

Trockenheit. A dry time.

I could take a bus, the man at the ticket desk tells me, or train, to complete my journey. But I don't want to take a bus. I want to take the boat, as Lawrence did. As we had done. Or if not, to walk. I find a seat on the upper deck towards the back. There's plenty of space. The boat leaves exactly on time. And it's surprisingly hot already. White birds wheel. The sun gleams on the open water. The Rhine is wider and bluer than I recalled. Our minds were elsewhere that morning, no doubt. Bathers bob near the banks, men in small boats are hunched over fishing rods. The steamer chugs from one fairy-tale village to the next: pointed red roofs and frescoed facades. Around me people stand up to take photos. Then sit down. Stand up. Sit down.

So Lawrence was alone on this trip?

It had been chilly that day and I remember having this conversation over coffee in the cabin.

Frieda was visiting her family. In Baden. She and Bert had arranged to meet up in Milan.

Julia was the professor of literature. Not me. She had won a grant to research Lawrence's psycho environmentalism. Or metaphysical environmentalism. There was some jargon term.

Funny, I said, to think of two such passionate lovers being out of touch.

For four years and nine months no day had passed without our exchanging scores of messages.

Imagine if we published them! she laughed. She had pulled up her hood on deck and now she shook out her hair and we kissed. Of course, she thought, if they'd had phones, they would have done the same, wouldn't they? She had the pages of Lawrence's account of his trip in her bag, torn from a book, and occasionally read a line as we watched the old villages come and go through spots of rain on the window. Ermatingen, Reichenau. *The poignancy of the past*, she read, *was almost unbearable, floating in colour upon the haze of the river.*

There is no haze this morning. A waiter is serving café crèmes on deck. With sticky pastries. And as the morning passes, I must say my heart lifts. The air is so fresh, the throb of the engine soft and easeful. A cloud of swans glide over their reflections. Two blimps dawdle in the sky. Whatever your reasons for making this journey, I tell myself, it seems you have done the right thing. The world is more friendly than you think, Mr Burrow. The coffee delicious.

All the same, as we proceed along the river – and now there are wooded slopes and sometimes vineyards – the thought of those messages rankles. Good morning, my love. The tiny screen of the old grey Nokia. Good morning beautiful. Just chasing the kids off to school. Lunch with Rachel today. Thinking about the corner of your mouth. Peter is away Thursday. The curve of your back. Why do you wear such boring shirts! Fraid I have an exam at three. Catherine is acting up again. Are you in a meeting? The body mist, not the perfume. It's raining here. Can't wait to be with you. Tomorrow at Caffè Nero. Sleep tight, Beautiful. Don't dream anything I wouldn't.

Four years and nine months. Three hundred and sixty-five times four, plus nine times thirty. One thousand six hundred, seven hundred? Times twenty. At least twenty. Maybe double that. Fifty thousand a conservative estimate? You're so conservative! She pinched my cheek. How Bert Lawrence would have made fun of you!

But it's getting seriously hot on the upper deck. The sun is relentless. I walk down to the cabin where everything feels uncannily familiar: a kitchen hatch at one end and meals being served. Could it be the same boat? By the door two men are sitting over beers, intent on a game of cards. They keep their hands tight to their chests.

We should turn our phones off, I told her.

This trip would mark the end of the phone era. From now on we would say good morning in the flesh.

There might be calls from the university, she thought.

I sit and order a beer myself. It's strange, watching the card players, how their cheerful being together has to do with hiding things from each other. An ace, a joker. *Scheisse!* one man cries.

If I turn off the phone, she thought, it might seem I have something to be afraid of. We were sitting across the table from each other, a varnished wooden table, screwed to the floor. Like this one. The surface sticky. She took my hand, laid it palm down, placed hers above, then my other hand above hers, then her other above that. I pulled out my bottom hand and slapped it on top. Then she, then me. Faster and faster. Who could keep their hand on top? Until we were laughing out loud.

You'll miss sending messages, she told me.

I shook my head.

You always write such lovely, loving things.

I will not miss sending messages.

I distinctly remember saying those exact words to Julia in the cabin of the steamer, somewhere between Konstanz and Schaffhausen. She really did have to be available to discuss students' grades, she said. *C'est la vie.*

In the cabin a bit of a scene is developing at one of the tables: parents remonstrating with a girl who pushes her plate away and goes to stand at the window. A boy gets up to plead with her. Her younger brother? She must be sixteenish. Other diners are pretending not to notice.

I drain my beer and go out on the lower deck. The boat is approaching Steckborn. Another pretty riverside village, with its Hotel Alte Post. Of course the name rang a bell! The world once revolved around the tavern where the post-chaise would stop, the driver sound his horn, the locals come running. The message from far away is so exciting.

Julia's phone vibrated. She never used the ringtone. But to me the low throb came loud as a klaxon.

Dean's office, she said. For heaven's sake, Dan.

I love the approach manoeuvre, how the steamer reverses its paddles and the water foams. Birds flapping away. Two of the crew, man and woman, stand by with their ropes, their white caps. The wooden pilings of the landing stage are cracked and slimy. The man has missed his throw and gathers his rope to toss it again. The woman laughs and ties off a hitch with gloved hands. Timbers creaking as the boat is hauled alongside, the gangplank thrust across the gap.

It's a lively scene in hot sunshine. First the passengers on foot, then the cyclists, leaving the boat, joining the boat. With their little backpacks, their helmets. Calling to each other, in German. Julia was one of the first to start wearing a helmet, when they seemed the merest fad. You admire Lawrence so much for being bold and adventurous, I teased, for running off with another man's wife, then you wear a helmet for a ride in the park. But she couldn't see it: it was one thing to be romantically bold and quite another to be careless. You should wear one too, she told me. I don't want to be the person calling the ambulance when you split your skull on the kerb. Headmaster Dies, she sang out, crossing Kew Bridge with Mistress! I don't text while I ride, I said. Also, she added, you wouldn't be so recognisable in a helmet. The famous forelock would be hidden. Crestfallen, I offered. We laughed and I bought my helmet. But only wore it when I was with her.

Stein am Rhein is another gem. Cobbled marketplace and old stone fountain. Breast-plated soldier on a column. I'm struck by the grey and pink frescoes thronging a grand facade. Recently restored, by the looks of it. Owls, fish, fruit, a sundial. Like the tattoos everyone has these days. Or the airships in my room last night. The same silky retro. Though you have to wonder what sense it can make frescoing a sundial with the light always at the zenith? Like having north always at your elbow. Rachel's tattoo phase, I remember, picking up picnic stuff in a small supermarket, was also her time of maximum disorientation. Butterflies and roses and Celtic crosses. They all seemed like cries of help to me.

Enough. I cross a bridge blazing with petunias and start west along the path beside the river. For a while I'm extremely focused on the present, the map, the need to make it to my B&B before evening. For sure it's hot weather to be tramping about with a backpack. To my right, two girls are floating in the stream, hanging on to an airbed and drifting along more or less at my walking speed. Lots of people are doing it. Old and young. Floating down the river in couples or little groups, calling to each other and laughing. I hadn't expected the Swiss to be having so much fun. How do they get back to where they jumped in? The girls have been drifting along a good fifteen minutes now. Splashing about. A pink costume and a blue. Blonde and brunette. Now a little ahead of me, now a little behind, depending on the current, the meanders, my pace on the path. Their airbed is white. Eventually they wave. Across the water. They've become aware of me, marching beside them. One shouts. The blonde. Water glistening on bright skin. I can't understand. They're laughing, I'm sweating. I wave back. I wish I could drift down the river, letting myself go in the cool of the stream. It's twelve miles to Schaffhausen. Another two to Rhine Falls. Then three to Jestetten. What are you doing, I wonder, re-enacting our Lawrence trip? Our catastrophe. You haven't thought about this stuff in years. Two men and a boy are paddling upstream in an Indian canoe and the girls grab at the gunwales, one either side. Their shrieks are loud across the water. The men protesting. Then the path climbs steeply left, away from the river. A thick stand of maples hides the view. For a while I can hear their voices through the trees. Then I'm on my own, marching across a field of stubble. The ground is grey and hard under the hot sun. *Trockenheit*.

But is it true I haven't thought about it for years? Isn't there a way in which this trip has been there all the time? Life collects its background noises. The upsets and traumas. You get used to them and get on with it. Then a package arrives, forwarded from a previous address. Sadly, my mother has passed away. She left instructions to send these pages. And the noise is thunder again; but it always was. Finally you find yourself reading what you never previously bothered to: *When I went from Constance, it was on a small steamer down the Rhine to Schaffhausen* ... D. H. Lawrence. 1913.

There is no noise in this dry field. The silence is uncanny. A hawk is drifting in the upper air. Like the girls in the river, it seems to be keeping pace with me. A party of cyclists obliges me to stand aside a moment, but I'm the only walker out here. After the stubble there is just parched grassland. Mainly flat. Low hills in the distance.

Everything is parched and dry and flat. And surprisingly empty. Not a house in sight. *There is something very dead about this country*, Lawrence wrote. His pages surprised me. They weren't what I had imagined from how Julia spoke of him. And now another surprise is a mobile toilet. In the middle of nowhere, an upright blue-and-white plastic box. As if Doctor Who's Tardis had landed from a different time.

Despite having no need, I peek inside. Perhaps I can steer it back a decade or two. There's a waft of chemical heat. It's roasting in there. But perfectly clean, well maintained. Julia would have been appreciative. She hated having to go in the bushes. There's a website address and a toll-free number to call. In case the paper has run out, I suppose. I imagine a helicopter racing across the scorched earth to winch down the wherewithal. And I imagine laughing about this with Julia. We were always laughing. Glancing up, the hawk is still there, scanning the withered grass.

But I'm hungry now. I'm pouring sweat. Eventually a little path drops down to the right, through a steep thicket, back to the river. It's the kind of path people make by themselves, when there's a real urge to get somewhere. An unofficial path. I have to shift aside branches of bramble and trip over a root. At the bottom there's a stretch of mud and stones. The air hums with insects. I push my backpack under the shade of a willow. And yes it is the same backpack I used all those years ago. And my pocketknife, to slice my bread and cheese, is the same knife. But first I need to cool down.

I strip to my underwear and pick my way to the water's edge. You can see the river is low. Big flat pebbles coated in dry mud. There's still the occasional bather drifting by, voices calling. But it's more remote here; the river glides green and glassy between heavy trees that bow towards it. And it's moving fast. If I go in deep it will carry me off. If I stay on my feet I won't get cool. The sun is burning. You're so white, Julia protested. The only thing to do is to stretch out, on my stomach, in a foot of fast water, face to the current, fingers thrust into the mud to stay put. Then it's gloriously fresh. The water flows over me from head to toe. Taking the heat with it. And the sweat. For a few minutes I lie like this, inches from the riverbed, fingers digging in, chill water lapping at my chin, eyes watching the surface slide towards me. Upstream, someone is kneeling on a paddleboard, trying to get to her feet. Floundering, trying again. Already she's behind me. If I turn I'll lose my grip. Again I feel a desire to let go, let the Rhine carry me off. But then where would I be?

Where would we be, she said, if you did that?

What Lawrence had done, she meant: the letter to Frieda's husband announcing their love, burning their bridges.

Where they were, I suppose.

These were the first heady days. I wanted something to happen.

She shook her head: Lawrence didn't have to teach Frieda's children, did he?

I'll give up my job.

There's Catherine, she said.

I push my face down in the water, eyes closed. I would

13

never have done something that changed Julia's life without her consent. It was true her daughter Catherine was a constant worry. Yet, holding my breath now, in the cool river, I still have half a feeling that that was what she wanted, deep down: to have it over with, and not be responsible; if I had been man enough. As Lawrence was.

Coming up for air, there's a large white rowing boat with a party of picnickers. They have a bottle of wine. The oars are splashing. For a moment I let the boat swell to a small steamer. After all, we must have passed this way. Here it comes. Sounding its horn to warn the bathers. The bow wave sparkles. The beat of the paddles. Julia is at the cabin window but doesn't raise her head. She's looking at a message on her phone.

I get to my feet and pick my way across the stones. I never wrote that letter, of course, but what I did do, after a year or so, was buy two super-light state-of-the-art hiking packs. If you're going to research someone's reflections on the environment, I told her, you should at least do the same walk he did. We saw at once how this would provide the perfect excuse. But the packs were three years old before we lifted them onto our backs. By which time the Rhine had become our Rubicon.

It's wonderful how synthetics don't decay. After all its years in garage and attic, the blue fabric is still shiny. The zips all zip. My red pocketknife is still in the belt pouch, the blade still sharp. Slicing an apple, it occurs to me that I have never really got used to life. The things that stay with us and the things that pass. Despite the decades devoted to teaching. The things that become softer and smoother with time, and the things that start to smell bad. Nor do I know what happened to the photos we took. She took, rather. Do they still exist? Did anyone ever look at them?

I eat staring at the river. Object of countless lessons. The rift valley. The barge traffic. Cologne. Düsseldorf. Rotterdam. You're such a Boy Scout, Julia marvelled. Field trips, I told her. Best part of a geography teacher's life.

But now two boys have found their way down the path. They are sorting through their fishing gear. I need to break out of this mood. The heat is oppressive. Perhaps the day will come when the Rhine dries up and there are no more boats and no more bathers. Consulting Google, I see there is a train from Diessenhofen, not far away. It was at Schaffhausen, after all, that we started walking.

'Not very real'

I arrive in Jestetten later than planned, which adds a certain edge to my meeting with my landlady. I had booked
the only place available in the village, estimating my
arrival time at six p.m. But it's almost nine when I show
up. Everything has taken longer than expected. In particular, I wasted an hour trying to get a decent view of the
Rhine Falls without paying. We didn't have to pay to see
them years ago. Why should one pay to see a natural landscape feature? But all my attempts to get round the barri-
ers proved futile. The whole hillside has been fenced off.

Then the house, my B&B, is not actually in Jestetten, as
I supposed, but half a mile down a side road that tracks back
towards the Rhine. This is definitely not where we stayed
years ago. That was the Hotel Bahnhof, now closed for holidays its website says. Nor had Lawrence stayed here. He
walked ten miles further south, to Eglisau. But Julia was not
a walker and we had decided to ease into our hiking with
a mere six miles. There was no imperative to do the trip in
the same time Lawrence did. A long summer was before us
and after that our new lives together in the house I had
bought. We even took the time to board one of the tour boats

that creep up the wooded shore then break out into the turbulence under the great cascade so that you feel the deck lift under your feet with the force of the current. Peering through the links of the new fence, high up on the hill, I was able to watch as a red cruise boat crossed the broad pool beneath the falls, entered the stream and was thrust away, careering sideways down the river. But the falls themselves were hidden by the spur of the hill, beyond the fence.

The boat turned to approach the point again, moving from the dark water to the white so the tourists could have a second thrill. It was quite a big vessel with at least a hundred people aboard. Why do I find such things so mesmerising? Again, no sooner had it reached the frothing water than it was tossed aside like a toy under the bath tap, and I remembered how the first time we had felt that force – the PA had been warning us to hold on to a rail – Julia and I clutched at each other, frightened, laughing, happy.

Number 25 Siedlerstrasse, when I finally find it, is a low modern house surrounded by a brick wall. There are no bells so I push the gate and walk to the door. Here there is a bell; you can hear it ringing. No one answers. I set down my pack, which is beginning to chafe. The sun has fallen behind the hills, the shadows are lengthening. Now I'm impatient – I made this booking weeks ago, they have long since taken my money – yet also uneasy, as if I were trespassing.

Looking about me, I see that the garden path leads away to my right through lush shrubs and flower beds to another bungalow and another door. Leaving my pack where it is, I walk over there and ring a second bell. The door is glass, but the interior concealed with a blind that soon enough is tweaked aside to reveal a pale round face. The door doesn't open. I have a booking, I announce. I raise my voice. Mr Burrow. *Eine Buchung.*

The woman watches from drooping eyelids. She's alone, I suppose, and wary. In her forties. She had expected her guest three hours earlier. I'm sweaty, no doubt, tousled. Red from the sun. This is a holiday flat for four, situated in unremarkable countryside. A place for families. Germans or Swiss. Not foreign men, travelling alone. I was delayed, I explain. *Verspätet.* Eventually, the door opens a crack. Perhaps my age has reassured her. *Guten Abend, Herr Burrow. Wo ist Ihr Auto?*

In the train from Diessenhofen to Schaffhausen I had watched intently as the landscape slid by. Low empty hills. Beech trees. A harvester toiling along rows of maize. You always make things difficult for yourself, I reflected. As if you were afraid of having time on your hands. No one works the hours you do, Julia told me. No one in their right mind!

Schaffhausen is a larger, more stately version of Stein am Rhein, with ornate bay windows lining the main street. *Not very real*, Lawrence wrote. I remember Julia trying to explain to me what this odd pronouncement meant in his scheme of things. I found her admiration for the writer irksome at times, as if we were competitors for her affection. If a thing is not real, what is it? I asked. She chuckled. I was so categorical.

Eating an ice cream in the central square, I made a serious attempt to see Julia, really to stand face to face with her again. Straight nose, high forehead, the kind of hair you know must once have been red, worn in a tress, over the left shoulder. Strong jaw, mouth sharp with lipstick. But this was a photograph, the snap that inhabited my wallet for years. Not very real.

Seen on her own, standing in the street, tall, Junoesque – when we had arranged to meet, perhaps, and I caught sight of her before she me – she might appear rather solemn, absorbed in some other life. Or just plain glum, deep vertical lines either side of the lips. But when our eyes met, her face lit up with mischief. The cheeks lifted. Then she was almost too playful. There was something furtive as well. I loved that. She might tuck something away in her bag, as I approached. Or quickly close a phone call. A sudden change of expression. How intriguing it was! Her embrace was all breathy warmth. Wilfully voluptuous. So fabulous to see you, Dan.

All this I recalled, rather deliberately, even grimly, licking honey-almond ice cream under a bay window in Schaffhausen. The blue dress over the mature curve of the belly. Another photo. Bright eyes under a straw hat. It all felt pretty thin compared to any of the women, young and not so young, sauntering through the cobbled Haupstrasse on this summer afternoon. Or drinking through a straw at a café table. Slim fingers, silver nails. For a moment I felt stilled, baffled, as if by a sort of vertigo or dizziness. Where am I, what am I doing?

To reach the falls you have to negotiate a tangle of fast roads which I didn't recall from our previous trip. Then a mile and more along the north bank of the river until you cross a bridge – actually a pedestrian walkway beside railway lines – just a hundred yards or so before the stream plunges and turns south. I spent a while here, leaning on the rail. You can see the dark water whitening among the shoals as it slides and jostles towards the drop, hear the roar as it crashes down beyond. Whenever I see something like this, I told Julia, I can't help but imagine being down in there, drawn towards something I can't see. From time to time, as I watched, a mist of spray blew off the lip of the fall. The cheerful Mr Burrow, she observed.

Feeling a little foolish for not having paid to see the sight proper – when will I get another opportunity? – I lost my bearings and made a couple of false starts. We had used paper maps on the previous trip. Which direction had I come from? I turned the phone round and expanded things a bit. Eventually a path wound down a wooded slope to the river downstream of the fall. Cows loitered in the shade under leafy trees, taking refuge from the after-noon heat. They were big bony Swiss cows, light brown in colour, with patches of creamy white. Not unlike the ones I had risen at five to milk every morning, all those years ago, on the farm near Basel. Perhaps you are taking this walk, it suddenly occurred to me, to avoid some other decision. But what? At my age. And why think this now?

The cows chewed slowly, their rheumy eyes blank. And I smiled. The farmer had had four daughters. Grubehof, the place was called. Or perhaps Grubenhof. All very sweet and pretty. Just that the oldest was barely fifteen. Too young, I had thought. Laughing and playing round the farmyard all that summer, tanning themselves on the grassy bank above the water trough where a goat was tied, these girls fed an atmosphere of yearning that suddenly came back to me as I reached the river and a footbridge to the German side. There were children here too, boys and girls in their teens, jumping into the swirling water from the bank, climbing out and jumping in again.

What a pleasure that yearning had been! What an agony! Tugging the teats of the cows in the early morning to prepare them for the machine. Watching the first milk squirt. The farmhand I worked beside – Gerhard – seemed aware of my hankering and would endlessly croon a song whose refrain exploded on the word *Mädchen*, and then again *Strümpfen*. He grinned and slapped his hands on the back of his thighs, a childish fat-faced man who wore a leather cap and spoke harshly to his lame, lopsided wife. We cleaned out the shed, forking straw and shit onto a barrow, pushing brooms down a channel that frothed with piss beneath the animals' tails. Then to breakfast where the daughters, the *Mädchen*, warm and fragrant from their beds, would giggle over heaps of fried eggs, bowls of black cherries, the youngest running round the big table bare-foot, no *Strümpfe*, but poking fun at an older sister who had started wearing a bra, pulling up her own pyjama top, shrieking and pulling it down again, while the eldest of the four, Johanna, watched solemnly throughout, eating daintily, with the superior composure of her well-fed almost adult form.

Never once did she look my way. It seemed a sort of cosmic bad joke at the expense of a boy who already feared that he was a late starter, that he must do something soon. Until, one Sunday, after lunch – the only hours of respite from the cows – Anouk appeared. The niece. A city girl, from Basel. She wasn't beautiful, but she was seventeen and possessed a moped and a few words of English, both of which we used very soon to great effect. I lost my virginity, I remember explaining to Julia, who was always intensely curious about my past life, on a hillside under moonlight in the long grass beside a wood. Though technically I'm not quite sure that's true. Anouk had brought a groundsheet; we took off our clothes and embraced. It's happening, I thought. Suddenly there was a movement, a heavy thud. Startled, we shrank apart. From the dark of the trees a bullock shook its horns and stared.

Climbing through the woods beyond the river, I found myself in low evening sunshine on an open plateau where field after field of stubble had been ploughed back into the powdery earth. I saw Anouk three or four more times after that debacle and even spent a day with her, when my time at the farm was over, in Lausanne. But we never got naked again, perhaps for fear a horned animal would burst from the shadows. Why am I recalling this now? I wondered. Why am I not concentrating on that marvellous afternoon with Julia as our great escape began and we walked side by side, full of hope, free at last, on that easy stroll from Rhine Falls to Jestetten? We had a groundsheet of our own and lay down to eat a peach. I'm enjoying this, she announced. I do hope there's a restaurant in the village.

Is there a restaurant near by? I ask my landlady. She's in a great hurry to show me the flat and be gone. Here is the bathroom. The stove is induction. Wi-Fi code on the coffee table. Bin under the sink. She speaks in telegraphic

German, rubbing small nervous hands. Of course there are restaurants, Herr Burrow. The Café Central. The Bangkok Thai. I smile, but she is already at the door.

In the shower I marvel how luxurious water can be after a long hot walk. But again my mind goes back to the eyes staring from the trees. Fact is, I told Julia, I can't see a cow, even now, especially not a cow in a wood, without remembering that evening, and all I really see is that animal standing there shaking its horns, to the point I'm not even sure what happened between me and Anouk. Moo! Julia intoned as we made love. And we fell apart, helpless with laughter.

Comes a knock at the front door. *Hallo?* It opens a little. *Hallo?*

Yes.

I should tell you, Herr Burrow, those restaurants will close at ten.

Ah. It is almost nine thirty and I also am speaking through a barely open door, from the bathroom. Thank you.

But she waits for me to dress.

You are tired.

I have walked from Stein am Rhein.

Her eyes open a little. *Respekt!*

In the end she brings me a soup and salad. It would surely be easier to invite me to her kitchen and serve it there. But she prefers to carry the saucepan along the path between the two bungalows. She doesn't want me to see her private space, perhaps. And she sits at the end of the table while I eat. There's a candle, a red candle on a glass dish, for romantic guests, one presumes. Julia loved candles. She doesn't light it. Would I like a beer? She goes out again and stays away for some time before bringing back a bottle from which she pours a little for herself. She has a son, she says, studying in Birmingham. You have children?

A daughter. Unnecessarily, I add, My wife died when she was sixteen.

She sits watching me, attentively. Her son loves England, she says. Now he has an English girlfriend as well. I'm afraid he may decide to stay.

There are worse fates, I tell her, and I explain I'll be leaving very early in the morning. I need to get to bed. She won't hear of being paid for the supper. I watch through the window as she carries saucepan and salad bowl back across the dark garden. Then a security light comes on and only now do I notice that she is wearing a floral dress, with white and red roses. Should I have stayed at the table and chatted? You never notice what I'm wearing, Julia would chide. Sometimes I wondered how Julia could love me with all the things she chided me for. I was conservative, I was categorical, I dressed boringly, worked too many hours, believed in discipline and had no feeling for literature. Unless it was precisely the playful chiding she loved, and the thought that she was with someone she would never have dreamed of as a partner?

Dreams. In bed I'm fully expecting I'll dream of our story. Those momentous days when we were together at last. Instead, I dream the old dream of Margaret. That she hasn't died. Or she has, but it hardly makes much difference. The variation this time is that we keep a white salmon in the bath, a big silvery fish that allows itself to be fed and fondled. One of its fins has fallen off and we are trying to mend it with cooking foil. The salmon thrashes in the bathwater and another fin falls off. At the same time I am trying, on the sly, to text Julia and tell her we have a problem: My wife isn't dead! But my fingers are slimy with scales and instead of letters the screen fills with satellite images of rapidly moving weather patterns. Then I realise Rachel is watching from the bathroom door.

The quilt on the bed is too hot. Sweating, I strip off the cotton cover and try to get back to sleep under that. Julia loved to psychoanalyse. So you had trouble getting off the mark, she summarised, and as a result allowed an older woman to kidnap you. Of course, as soon as she's had the child she's desperate for she becomes jealous because she senses you would prefer a woman you chose yourself, a younger woman, not one who chose you. And she encourages your daughter to spy on you. I remember how extraordinary it felt, hearing this version of my life. Completely plausible, yet quite wrong.

Unable to sleep, I fish Lawrence's pages from the bottom of my pack. *I came on to a long, desolate high-road, with dreary, withered trees on either side, and flanked by great fields where groups of men and women were working. They looked at me as I went by down the long, long road, alone and exposed and out of the world.*

'A small, forgotten, wonderful world'

The plan is to be up and off at six, eating breakfast in the first café that presents itself. But no sooner have I turned on the bedroom light than there's that voice again, at the door, calling softly, *Hallo!* My landlady has brought a pot of fresh coffee and a fruit flan in a biscuit tin. So here we are once more sitting at the table with the red candle. Of course I'm glad to have something to eat, but impatient to be away. Through the windows, day is dawning. And I notice her eyes have a short-sighted, peering look as she follows me round the room. Was she wearing contact lenses yesterday? I'm always up early, she says. She seems happy to drink a coffee herself while I gather my few things. The forecast is for 38 degrees, she warns. It's not a day for walking. I've already booked a hotel in Zürich, I tell her, for tonight. Saying goodbye, we shake hands. There's a light dusting of freckles on the pale skin beneath her eyes. I feel the need to be gone.

Outside, the air is cool over dry white grass. Away to the left, the red roofs of Altenburg cluster around a spire. I know we walked the first miles along the river, but can't remember how we got back down there. It hardly matters. A path drops steeply through thickets of oak and bramble, a ruined cottage, a broken wall. It's still dark down here. If you stop there are distant snatches of birdsong. And a tense vegetable hush, a sort of drawn-out sigh before the coming heat. Where the path reaches the riverbank, an abandoned boathouse overhangs the water. It's rather a handsome thing, or was, a stone base with rotting wooden walkways either side. Waiting for renovation.

Was this where she told me she had had a message from Catherine? It's amazing how little I recall with precision. The first thing Julia would do when she woke of a morning was check her phone for messages. The first thing I did, the few nights we managed to spend together, was gauge whether she had got good news or bad. Or none. And this anxious attentiveness to her mood would irritate her. So I fought my desire to know, and my eagerness to have her to myself. Though it was that eagerness that gave her the strength to go on, she would say at other moments. I couldn't even dream of doing any of this, she would say, without you. But without you I would never have wanted to do it. After a happy evening at the Hotel Bahnhof, we walked in silence beside the Rhine, which is slow and still here, with weeds trailing below the surface and swans wraithlike in patches of mist. No doubt the water was higher then; it rained that summer.

Catherine texted, she said.

I thought they weren't allowed to use their phones at the retreat.

She shrugged.

Along the path there are people walking their dogs. A man on a bike with a Dobermann trotting after. Julia would sometimes stop to pat people's dogs while I stood and watched. You should feel how silky his ears are, she would turn her head to me. When she crouched, her dress would tighten at the haunches, her breasts spill forward. Such a cute damp little nose he's got, haven't you, my darling, haven't you? Oh, we have a love of a collie at home, she would say. A real love. He would have so much fun with you, he really would.

I hope the men are remembering to take Bobbie out, she worried now as we resumed our walk. She always referred to her husband and son as the men. Bobbie had often provided an excuse for our meeting.

So what did Catherine say? I asked.

After an hour or so the path climbs away from the river, then drops back down to it, then climbs again as the water slides into a gorge. The sun is well up now. There are handsome old farmhouses, balconies ablaze with white geraniums, cowsheds open on dark interiors, the animals stamping and shuffling in their shackles.

She sighed and spoke in a dull low voice. That I can't just disappear and abandon my husband and children.

I didn't know what to say. We walked in silence, stopping at a water trough to fill our bottles.

Anything from Rachel? she asked.

I reminded her I was keeping my phone off. I'd told Rachel I needed a break from parents and school governors. Julia complained that I made myself too available. These people should never have had my personal number in the first place.

We had been through this before. When people pay a

fortune, I rehearsed, to send their kids to school, they feel they have the right to call the headmaster twenty-four seven. I smiled: As someone we know once did.

Only I have the right, she cried! We embraced, backpacks and all. Her mouth was wide and soft. She kissed deeply. I let myself melt into her.

Consulting the map, I remember now that we had found a coffee in a place called Rüdlingen. Then instead of following the river in its long meander south, we climbed a steep hill due west, towards Eglisau, where Lawrence had spent the first night of his hike *in a great, lofty, old deserted house, with many drab doors.*

So I head that way now, through fields of pumpkins and turnips. The heavy orange fruit winks through tangles of leaves. The turnips are yellowish among dry clods and stones. There are tall stands of maize. The year is coming to fruition. Along the road, freshly cut logs have been stacked with obsessive precision. There's a well-swept Swissness to it all. Only, entering Rüdlingen, beside a big cowshed, a great heap of dung and straw is steaming in the sunshine.

I once fell into a pile like that, I told Julia.

I had noticed she loved anecdotes where I appeared clumsy and inept. Or where I said something dumb, or was just plain unlucky.

I can't find the café we stopped in. I seem to remember a handsome arch and a cobbled courtyard. Perhaps I'm mistaken. Instead, there's a tiny supermarket with a coffee machine by the till and tables outside. Two tables, one in the sun, one under a trellis of wisteria. I'll have to sit in the sun; the other is occupied.

We would fork the cow shit onto a sort of flat low barrow, I told her. Then you had to wheel the thing out of the shed and run it up a plank to the top of the dung pile. But shit is heavy and the barrow tipped from side to side. We worked in rubber boots, which are slippy on the wet. That morning it was pelting down. The plank was slimy with dung. I made my little run with the barrow, skidded near the top and went over in the pile with the shit on the barrow slithering down on top of me. At breakfast the girls couldn't stop giggling.

Kommen Sie doch hierher, says a voice. *Hier ist Platz. Hier ist Platz.*

The elderly man in the shade has seen I'm sweating. He moves up a little on his bench.

Dankeschön.

To be out of the sunshine, I have to tuck in on his side of the table. He's dressed quite smartly in a light suit and blue shirt. Thinning white hair neatly parted. I sip my coffee. He has finished his, but still holds his cup in mottled hands. Our closeness makes the silence embarrassing.

It's quiet here.

He bends a hand round his ear.

I raise my voice: There's no one about! No one in the shop either.

He nods. Everyone on holiday. Summer.

And you?

His cheeks are veined but the eyes strikingly clear. I'm too old for holidays, he says.

He is watching me as I drink. He's not going to ask a question. At the same time he seems sympathetic, intrigued. As if there were something surprising about me. A wasp hovers over the tabletop.

Perhaps I'm too old for holidays too, I smile. *Zu alt für Ferien*, I repeat a little louder. *Ich auch.*

He asks where I am going.

Eglisau.

You are English.

Yes.

He gets to his feet, slowly. He has a walking stick that he uses to push himself erect. Then he looks at me frankly, in a kind of fond farewell, as if we had been speaking for some time. In throaty English he says: You are not old, sir! Enjoy your walk.

Climbing out of the village, I come across the café where we stopped. Hens are pecking on the cobbles and a van is parked in the courtyard. It must have closed years ago. We had sat in the corner, I remember, on the left, and before leaving Julia had unbuttoned the top of her shirt to show me where her pack was rubbing on her collar bones. I cut plasters and applied them with a dab of Savlon above breasts pressed into a shiny sports bra, her breath on my hair as I spread the cream. But it's impossible to recover the excitement of those days. Why, I asked, are you always so pleased when I make a fool of myself?

You really don't know? She mussed my hair.

The path climbs steeply now through dry vineyards and far below you can see the river, in its gorge, circling the hill, the water a startling turquoise where it catches the sun.

I've no idea, I told her. Not that I mind. I just noticed.

She laughed remembering the account her children had

31

given her of how I tripped over the microphone cable at the year's prize giving.

But why is it so funny?

She stopped to take a breather. It was our first real climb. Up above you could see a church with a patterned spire, red and green.

Someone screwing up is endearing, she said.

We started walking again. At a certain point the path turns into a flight of steps.

It's like suddenly you're a little boy. Which is sweet. While in reality you're quite intimidating.

Oh, come on.

No, you are! She was serious, even emphatic. Head-master of a posh private school. All the pupils look up to you. The parents trust you. Pillar of the establishment. Authoritative.

You're joking.

Even on this trip. You know everything about hiking. About boots and backpacks. About the Rhine. Geology. River steamers. You've got the maps sorted. The hotels. You even speak German! As soon as I have a little sore you whip out plasters, Savlon and mini-scissors!

It's just a first aid kit.

It's monstrous.

I felt baffled. But you're a professor, Julia! How impres-sive is that? Geographers are all jocks and rocks. No one takes us seriously.

She stopped on the step below me, breathing hard. And burst into tears. She buried her head in my chest. Be strong for me, Dan. I need a rock. I need strength. Really.

The clocks on Swiss churches are larger than in other countries. I'm convinced of that. Their faces and hands more brightly painted. Blue and gold in this case. It's 10.15. In each vineyard I climb through, a notice informs me of the name of the winegrower, the variety of grape, the exact number of vines, the year of planting. I can't recall seeing this kind of thing in the countryside before. Another notice tells me that the fruit is insured against hailstorms; there's the name and phone number of an insurance company. In the lane, beyond Buchberg church, every farmhouse carries dates in Gothic script, below the eaves or beside the door: when it was built, when it was renovated. An old winepress is displayed in the street, with a long explanatory caption, as if the whole world were a museum. The Swiss flag is everywhere. Square white cross on red background. Draped over a balcony. Hanging limp from a pole in a garden. Perhaps Lawrence was on to something, I reflect, wandering through Europe to capture the mood. In Eglisau I encouraged Julia to talk about her research. Ecocriticism – that's the term – in pre-war literature. It was only when she talked about her work that she seemed able to put her maternal anxieties aside.

The two miles from Buchberg to Eglisau are easy walking. Open fields, distant hills and woods, the drone of a chainsaw. I can't remember it being anywhere like this hot the day we did it. Just before the path turns down to the river and the old town, there is a campsite. Four neat rows of dormitory tents with a great white wigwam in the centre. Field trip, is my first thought. Then I see some men in khaki.

She started to talk. We had found a café at the top of the town with a long wooden balcony overlooking the village and the strangely blue-green river. *A small, forgotten, wonderful world*, Lawrence wrote. He was fascinated, she explained, but also appalled by the way an age-old intimacy with the land and its rhythms was being replaced by what he called the mechanical money principle. It had been a stroke of genius on my part, I thought, to have combined our escape with her research. We sipped Apfelschorle and ate trout. It wasn't just an anti-capitalist rant, she insisted, it was a *cri de coeur*.

The paths down into the town are precipitous, the views magnificent. More vines, more steps. In the distance, a viaduct crosses the river. My right knee is playing up and I have to take it slowly. On the wall of a fine old house – 1670, restored 1993 – are two cartoon figures. An orange Roger Rabbit, a blue Mickey Mouse. With names and dates. Gabriel 2/4/2019. Mila 8/11/2017. They're not the first I've seen. One house has Daffy Duck and Yogi Bear with birth dates in 2004 and 2008. Kids the same ages now as Julia's children were then. More or less. You wonder what a teenager is supposed to think, seeing himself forever Daffy Duck. This time I find the café at once. It is exactly as I remembered, a gloomy panelled lounge with French windows opening onto the bright sunshine of the balcony. But it's too early for lunch and I suddenly feel oppressed. Catherine was always our number one obstacle. Far more than her father. On the other hand, it was Catherine who had brought us together. I drink an Apfelsaft at the bar from a glass that has a tiny

Swiss flag on the side, then head down to the river for a swim.

This too is as I remember it. A greensward with a scatter of people lying on towels. You can dive in from the bank and let the current pull you along, a hundred yards or so, to the stone steps that come up by the old church. How many times did I answer calls from parents complaining that their children were being unfairly disciplined? In Catherine's case, suspended. By all means come to my office, was the stock response. Then I would consult our files. The girl's father was a stockbroker. She had a younger brother in Year 9. I discussed the matter with the teacher involved. Teachers, rather. What your daughter did was extremely dangerous, Mrs Ingram. Putting her own life and others at risk.

It was meant as a game, Headmaster, there was no ill intention.

I'm afraid Catherine's reaction to her teacher's objections was unacceptable. Shall I read you the report?

In the river I duck beneath the surface and swim a little way underwater. It's surprisingly clean. You can make out pebbles on the riverbed. A block of cement with a rusty hook. How long can I hold my breath? I used to be good at this. No longer. I'm forced up, gasping for air.

This was Catherine's game.

You and your husband were contacted before half-term, when she fainted during maths. Another girl had to go home sick.

Catherine has problems with maths.

Julia Ingram sat upright the other side of my desk.

Aside from the moment when we shook hands, I hadn't really looked at her yet. One tries to impose an atmosphere of cordial formality.

You were sent our psychologist's opinion. A serious form of self-harm. That is worrying enough. But when other children are drawn in it is quite unacceptable.

She started to reply, stopped and simply looked at me. I was obliged to meet her eyes. They were bright, pleading. I say this now, without seeing them. For some reason Julia's face never really appears to me. Even in dreams. But I do sense a sort of vibrancy, a pressure of persuasion across the years.

Catherine is top of her class, she said. In everything but maths. She's a credit to the school. All she was doing was holding her breath.

A boy was taken to hospital with concussion, Mrs Ingram.

I haven't recalled this scene in twenty years: the lovers' beloved first meeting. But Eglisau seems the right place to do it, where she talked so earnestly about Lawrence and we swam in the river, smiling faces in the water, and dried off on the grass, chuckling at the eager English of a German boy chatting up a foreign girl, then studied our maps and kissed and twined our fingers and Julia relaxed and said Catherine would get over it as kids invariably do, if anything it was her men she should be worried about, John particularly; in any event, she wasn't going to start banging her head against the wall as Frieda had done because she couldn't see her children.

Who would ever stop you from seeing them? I asked. They're grown up now!

Drying off myself, a little dazed from my underwater swim, I feel a sudden urge to call Rachel and start to rummage in my pack for my phone. All around me people are enjoying the summer midday, spreading picnics on groundsheets, running after toddlers. But I don't make the call. Rachel knows nothing of this part of my life.

Dear Mr Burrow, as we agreed, my daughter is not well. Words to that effect. The email will still be there, no doubt, on the school's server. Catherine was seeing a healthcare professional, she wrote. That expression was already in vogue. An eating disorder had been diagnosed, but this was now under control. Could she be allowed a *trial* return to school? I can vouch for her behaviour. Sincerely, Julia Ingram. And a PS: Forgive my impertinence, Mr Burrow, but during our conversation there was a drawing on the wall behind you that intrigued me. A woman's face, with a dog. Your mother, perhaps. I felt touched.

I sit down under a sunshade at a restaurant beside the river, but the waiter is slow to come and I'm eager to be off. Thinking is less dangerous on the move. There's a rather stylised stag painted on the white wall above me. The truth is that you love tiring yourself out, Julia complained, like you love working long hours. Finally the waiter brings a menu, and hurries off. While I don't, she said. I don't want to annihilate myself. Lawrence must have enjoyed tiring himself out, I objected, considering the kind of ground he was covering every day! Lawrence was manic, she laughed.

It's ten minutes before the waiter returns to take my order. Why are you so angry and tense? I wonder. I will raise the matter at tomorrow's staff meeting, I answered her mail. The drawing is of my late wife. Made by our daughter, Rachel, who is studying at art school.

My food isn't arriving. I can't catch the waiter's eye. When I do, he's brusque. *Es kommt, es kommt.* I'm so sorry, she apologised. She had phoned to thank me for cancelling Catherine's suspension. I hope I didn't cause you pain. Just that the drawing caught my eye. Margaret died a year ago, I told her, before I came to London. There's no way you could have known. No, I must apologise, she repeated. There was a silence on the line. I've been sitting here half an hour and still haven't been served. The heat is more oppressive by the minute.

I still remember that long silence, over the phone. Like this morning's hush before sunrise perhaps. To be fanciful. You're not from here, are you? she eventually asked. Ah, I relaxed, is it so obvious? The north somewhere? she guessed. I'm not good with accents. And a moment later she said, I do hope you have friends in London, Headmaster; it can be pretty grim here otherwise. Our story had begun.

And I've reduced my beermat to shreds. How long can it take to cook a schnitzel? I pick up my pack and I'm off. The hell with them. I march along the riverside, where the flower beds are frothing colour. Eglisau is a postcard. *A glamorous world*, Lawrence thought. I want out of the place. I want to walk all day.

'Like a blight . . .'

The novelty of hiking with Julia, I remember, crossing the bridge and putting the Rhine behind me, was seeing her in practical clothes. Julia loved to be feminine, in heels and pretty dresses; even cycling she was always made up and saw no contradiction between this and her feminism. But I insisted she buy boots for Switzerland. And proper trekking socks. It came on to rain that afternoon on the rolling country south of the river and her nose poked from the hood of her red cape. We pulled the waterproofs over our packs and held hands, bulky and damp, talking about D. H. Lawrence as we trudged. *Ordinary* was still his objection to this part of the country, *a horrible, average, vigorous ordinariness, like a blight*. Like Peter, Julia cried, that's what we're escaping. Ordinariness, he's so nice and busy and ordinary.

I start up the hill beyond the river in the fierce heat, feeling hungry now and remembering my landlady's warning. Had she wanted me to stay, perhaps? In her B&B in Jestetten? Ordinariness seems rather attractive here, I decide, admiring well-appointed modern homes, a stone wall topped with lobelia, thick hedges, polished cars. The road has stopped climbing now. There are more cartoon figures celebrating new arrivals: Goofy, the Lion King. As if children came from Disneyland. And again everything is numbered, catalogued. Lamp posts. Fire hydrants. A bin for dog shit. There are codes and acronyms. Even some of the trees have tags. *Akazie. Trauerweide.*

I'm rather looking forward to an ordinary life with you, I told her.

Contrarian! she protested. You pretend not to understand on purpose!

Julia would always insist that her marriage had been fine until she started seeing me. Fine in the sense of ordinary. She was under a spell, she would say, of ordinariness. Life was so hypnotically dull with Peter.

But now I'm falling under the spell of the heat. The sun is directly overhead. I've forgotten to fill my water bottle. How stupid can you get? I need to find shade and the only trees are in private gardens. I can't remember feeling this sort of weary weakness before, this taste of blood in the mouth. There is a promise of woodland on the hills up ahead. But how far away? I quicken my pace. Or try to. I'm short of breath. It's as if there weren't enough air. I should have eaten is the truth. Just lifting one foot after another is a struggle. I need to drink. Struggling at art school, is what I should have said of Rachel. Not studying. Lost at art school. Where is her famous drawing now? She gave it to me the Christmas after Margaret's death. The motherly face gazing wistfully at the viewer while a doggy snout stretches up to nuzzle her chin. The girl had talent. I see Margaret more clearly than I see Julia. Even in this sun-dazed state. My dead wife in our daughter's drawing. Where the viewer this unhappy woman is gazing at with such melancholy reproach is, of course, me. She crashed the car on purpose, Rachel said.

Suddenly I'm down on the pavement. Head spinning. Damn. I've cut my hand. *Sind Sie okay?* An engine is ticking over, close by. *Ja, ja.* Let me help. It's a woman's voice. *Dankeschön.* Or voices. There are a few bewildered moments, stumbling and clutching, then I'm sitting with my back to a tree, drinking from a glass. No, I'm sitting on a bench. I'm in someone's garden. A bench under a bower. A wooden table with a jug of water. Tinkling ice. Thank you so much, I'm okay. No, really.

We found these, sir. It is a man speaking now.

My sunglasses. Thank you, thank you. You're very kind.

The icy water goes down and at once the world is back again, stable and ordinary. We're under an awning by a whitewashed wall, surrounded with pots and flowers, a wrought-iron raven. To my left a black SUV is sitting on the gravel drive.

Where are you going, if I can ask?

I have a hotel in Zürich this evening. At some point I'll catch a train.

The two confer. Lawrence walked to Oerlikon, thirteen miles south of Eglisau. Then caught a tram. But in those days there was no international airport to get round. Julia and I had taken the train from Bülach, just five miles from here.

It is not a normal tourist . . . *Weg,* the woman observes.

41

The couple must be in their fifties. Wearing summery linen. From a window comes the sound of radio news.

I'm following a historic route, I explain, that someone once took, in 1913.

A younger woman comes out of the house with a bowl of fruit. Red shorts, white T-shirt. She has a plum in her mouth. Walks barefoot.

Please. Take. Go on.

I bite into an apricot, fridge fresh and intensely sweet.

I don't know who made this route, the man observes, but you are walking this way now, today, yes? Not in the past. He smiles. And today is very hot, yes? Very . . . unusual. If you will wait, my daughter is going to Eglisau. She can drive you to the station.

I'm fine, I tell them. Really, I just tripped.

I do feel absolutely fine. I take a second apricot. But I'm struck by what he said. And the whole afternoon, walking to Bülach, taking more care now, I keep repeating those words to myself. You're walking today, not in the past. There's a station at Glattfelden, the woman had said. You can catch a train there. But by the time I reach the turnoff for Glattfelden I'm only a few minutes from the woods. And I have a full water bottle again, and a big bag of plums. People can be surprisingly kind.

Beyond a busy roundabout a dirt road leads off the main thoroughfare to the left. There are a couple of caravans. A woman is sitting in the shade mixing something in a bowl. A dog runs back and forth along a wire, snarling. I hurry by. Then suddenly I'm in a place I recognise. The effect is that of a key turning in a lock. It's the long

42

track through the woods where it came on to rain and we donned our capes and sang as we marched. Stupid songs and sacred. 'On Ilkley Moor Baht 'at'. 'Jerusalem'. Anything. It was good to hear her singing voice, full and very deep. Full of life. Bring me my arrows of desire. The water trickling down our capes. You're walking today, not in the past. And today the air is warm and heavy and still. But if it weren't for the past you wouldn't be here at all. There is nothing for you here: an expanse of deciduous woodland, flat now. Splashes of sunshine through dusty foliage. Signs of forestry activity. Trees marked for culling. Small clearings with broken stumps. Logs piled under tarpaulins. All numbered.

It's impossible, of course, with all the tangled conversations of those days, those years, each alike as one tree to the next, each different in its ramifications, to recall when this or that was finally said, or unsaid, said for the first time, or the last, as we grew together and pushed towards the light. Tramping through the silent wood – but intermittently, to our right, there was the rumble of the main Zürich–Schaffhausen road, and always the patter of rain on an ocean of leaves – we sang 'Help!' and 'Let it Bleed' and 'Guide me Oh Thou Great Jehovah'. And talked. On our return we would go to live in the house I had just moved into, just bought for the purpose, in Chiswick. The children had been told that she was leaving her husband, their father, Peter Ingram, respectable stockbroker, hailing from an old and wealthy family with roots that went back to a certain Italian banker, Folco Inghirami, in the fourteenth century. But not that she had another relationship.

So the question was, when to tell Catherine and John that she was leaving him to live with me, Daniel Burrow, whose roots went no further than a shipyard supervisor at Birkenhead, my great-grandfather. But of course Daniel Burrow was also their headmaster, and occasionally, if someone was off sick and no adequate substitute could be found, their teacher, in the expensive school their father was paying for them to attend. To give them a better start in life. Or rather, had already paid for them to attend. They had finished. We had waited till her children finished school. My school. Catherine two years ago. John two weeks ago, stepping up to the podium to shake his headmaster's hand and carry off the Maths Prize. When to tell them, then, that this man up on the dais making speeches and offering congratulations was their mother's lover and had bought a house big enough for them to live in, should they so desire? Having reached their majority now. Albeit requiring some renovation work. Do I tell them separately or together? Julia agonised. And once told, how could they not realise, I worried, that Daniel Burrow had been their mother's lover while also their headmaster, guarantor of order and discipline, in all the years they had watched their parents' relationship come apart? They are bound to think that, aren't they? Bound to feel they have been tricked. But she denied it.

You are walking to Bülach in the uncannily hot summer of 2022, I remind myself, not in the pattering rain, of . . . What year was it? I can't recall. But I am absolutely certain we walked along this track. The moment I left the main road and the caravans, a key turned and I knew the place.

So many locks, perhaps, waiting in one's head for keys to turn them. As when you stand at the Arrivals Gate to greet the loved one you haven't seen in years. Will I recognise her? Will I? Then, yes, there in the jostling crowd, the one face that can unlock the floodgates. But of Julia not even a photograph. All destroyed and deleted. What's a lock without a key to turn it? I don't regret destroying them. It was a question of sanity. You are walking this path today, with the hot sun pressuring the leaves overhead, the air dry and warm and close. Not in the fine drizzle of years ago, kissing rain-wet lips, singing and talking, the back and forth of our decisions and indecisions, the excitement of feeling that after our years in the wilderness, we were close to the point where the trees thin at last, and you can step out onto the open slopes that lead to the mountain passes. You can breathe. John had been sent to a camp in Maine, for nine weeks. Catherine was serving in a Buddhist retreat. We were free.

Julia denied that her children had witnessed a slow decline in their parents' relationship. I couldn't understand her marriage, she told me. I shouldn't even try. She had been in analysis for years trying to understand why she had married Peter, very young, why she was still married to Peter. To no avail. You might as well try to explain, she said, why you were born into this family rather than that. Marriage had seemed the natural thing to do. The ordinary thing, that is. She understood perfectly what Lawrence meant when he spoke of an ordinariness that is almost a blight, referring to the countryside I am walking through now. Mile after mile of trees. All the same species.

Chestnut. Planted about six feet apart. In rows. For easy culling. The logs stacked under tarpaulins all along the track. Perhaps it was this detail that turned the lock, all these log piles old and new beside the track, under blue tarpaulin. Irreproachably neat. All these brownish green trunks, waiting to be cut down. Very occasionally, as I pass by, a rustle of dry leaves betrays an animal. A hedgehog perhaps. Very occasionally, there's a chirrup of birdsong. I remember in the rain together we had glimpsed a deer, far ahead on the dirt track that passes straight as a blade through this wood. A wood planted and managed, as regular notices remind me, by the Schweizerischer Forstverein. You could never lose yourself in this wood. There is only one track, always the same, arrow straight. With the hum of the Zürich–Schaffhausen road a few hundred yards to the right. Her marriage was always the same, Julia said, friendly, functional, she hadn't thought there was anything wrong with it. Just that when we had started seeing each other it ceased to be what she wanted. She had always had her freedoms, she explained. Peter had never been possessive. Always spent evenings, even occasional holidays, with her friends, apart from her family. Which was what made our affair so easy, of course. To me it seemed extraordinary that I could have had this effect on a woman. So easy to hide, I mean. For four crazy years. And nine months.

Look! she said. She squeezed my hand. The deer was thirty yards away in the middle of the path, front feet splayed, head slightly cocked, watching. What a beauty! She tried to find her camera, but it was in a pocket under

46

her cape. She fumbled. The animal turned and trotted away, lost in the trees. The moment I found you I didn't want to lose you, she said. No one had ever flattered me like this. She knew exactly what Lawrence meant, she said, when he spoke of a *vigorous ordinariness*. Peter was a vigorous man. You might even call him a jolly man, she thought. It was never difficult being around Peter. Not even after our affair had begun. Why should it be? I never felt I was betraying him. Can you betray ordinariness?

Still, he feels betrayed, I objected. You said so yourself. And I meant, by her request, some weeks ago, for a separation.

Not betrayed, bewildered, she said. Bewildered that something out of the ordinary had happened. It wasn't a sentimental loss, she thought, for her husband, when she told him she felt suffocated in their marriage, it was simply inexplicable. He had never known passion. An inexplicable fall in the stock market. As if a stranger had slapped him in the face. Ten years of analysis and she still hadn't understood why she had married him. But she had been so young. She had no idea. You might as well ask why there was this or that tree in the garden. Her children hadn't witnessed a slow decline. Because her husband refused to recognise that anything was wrong, that the ordinariness was over, the straight path had forked. Hence her difficulty telling the children. They had seen no change. Hence Catherine's fury: You can't just abandon your husband and children. It was a bolt from the blue.

I am walking this path from Eglisau to Bülach today, under a hot blue sky, but with the shade of the trees that will be with me almost to the end, almost to Bülach, and the stacks of timber on each side. When do they take the stuff away? you wonder. Some of the logs seem grey with age. Are they left here to weather? It's the kind of thing a geography teacher should know. Sometimes there's the whine of a beetle. The air is very still. Now a mill of tiny flies are fussing around my eyes. No people, though. I haven't met a single soul on this long straight track. And I can't recall we met anyone then, years ago, singing songs and hymns, tramping along in the drizzle, wondering how we might smooth over the move into the new house that I had bought, at great expense. Thinking of the renovation work that needed doing there.

But we had been talking about this for months, years. By this point I was entirely focused on the practicalities. I no longer hazarded my doubts about her version of her marriage. I no longer expressed my disbelief that her children could have failed to notice the change in their mother's life. Certainly Rachel noticed the change in mine. Who is it, Dad? she asked. I'm not criticising, she said. But she was criticising and I denied it. It was too soon after Margaret's death. She didn't ask again. My daughter didn't wash her hands of me exactly, in the years of my affair with Julia, just slowly detached herself from her father's world, her parents' world, the trauma of her mother's accident. After a long depression, she chose the path to independence and sanity. Good for her, Julia applauded. And so will Catherine, sooner or later.

I stop for a slug of water. There's a log to sit on and a strong smell of resin in the air. This timber has been recently cut. I eat the last of the plums. Opening the map on the phone, I see I'm nearly there. Another half-mile and I'll be out of the wood. Its shade has saved the day, but the monotony is beginning to pall. Forty-five minutes to Bülach station, Google calculates.

This wood's going on for ever, Julia sighed. It was our first full day's walking. The drizzle hadn't let up. Under our capes we were sweating. But I hadn't wanted to pull out our paper maps, in the rain. The path was straight. Even when it reached the road, the direction was always the same, due south to Bülach. Abide with me, Julia began to sing. In a deep alto voice. Fast falls the eventide. Did Lawrence use a map? I asked. He had picked windfall apples, she said, leaving Eglisau. Mushrooms in the woods. And eaten them too. Which was brave. But she couldn't remember his mentioning a map. He used the main roads; there was only the occasional horse and cart in those days. And asked people the way. He loved talking to people.

Even when he found them ordinary?

She laughed. In the hotel in Eglisau Lawrence had watched the proprietor feed a dozen unemployed men who had vouchers from the authorities for free room and board. In a tavern in Adliswil he talked to a group of expat Italian factory workers who met there for amateur theatricals. All these people, he thought, were victims of the mechanical money principle which devastated the countryside, fencing it in, asphalting and quarrying. These ideas sounded naïve to me, but once again our families were forgotten.

At last the path leaves the wood and drops down from

49

the plateau. You're in a modern industrial estate, where workshops and warehouses seem built of Lego, colourful and innocuous. You feel you could pick them up and move them around. Anywhere in the world. Flags are flying over a car salesroom. A container truck reverses alongside a loading bay. Then industry gives way to housing. At four thirty I grab a quiche and chips at a takeaway opposite Bülach station and eat on the platform waiting for my train. The metal seat of the bench is hot from the sun and as I try to get bits of quiche in my mouth without losing crumbs on my clothes, a woman paces up and down in front of me, speaking on her phone. She's the only other person on the platform, and she's speaking angrily, intently, holding her phone with arm outstretched as if afraid it might contaminate her. I can't follow what she's saying. In her thirties perhaps. She leaves no spaces for reply. Pacing back and forth like an animal. Griping, fretting, chiding. A powder-blue skirt. Now just a yard or so in front of me, now close behind. Her voice never stops. As I try to eat. Her lips working hard, free hand gesticulating, heels scraping on the platform. How can she be so self-absorbed, I wonder, as not to see I'm here?

'A most ordinary, average, usual person'

That night I had to wake Julia from an unpleasant dream. Tonight I can hardly sleep at all in this small stifling room. It must have had the sun all afternoon. There's no air-conditioning. I have been penny pinching, is the truth, booking the cheapest possible accommodation, but I'll only be in the city a few hours. Remarkably, there is no Reception in this place. They send you a code by email and you retrieve a key from a box beside the door. Inside, everything is spartan, but functional. If the weather were not so exceptional, there would be nothing to complain about.

Lawrence did not stay the night in Zürich, Julia explained. He took a steamer for a couple of stops and climbed a hill. But we wanted to see the town. We walked along the river from the station, checked in to a four-star hotel, showered, and enjoyed the happiest of evenings, wandering around the ancient streets, window-shopping, eating, drinking, laughing, then back to our room to make love. If ever I wondered why I had got myself into this, a relationship with a married woman whose children studied at my school, whose elder daughter showed every sign of a severe personality disorder, this was it: how much we enjoyed each other's company, how much we revelled in each other's flesh. I in hers, and she, to my astonishment, in mine. Even now, throwing open the narrow window of my tiny room over a grubby inner courtyard where two men are rolling beer barrels into the cellar of the pub beneath, a sound like rumbling thunder, even now, if I ask myself why on earth I am undertaking this odd, exhausting expedition, at my age, when there would be so many other pleasant things to do, the answer has to be the same: this was the one time in my life I felt transformed, by love, by passion. Old yearnings were fulfilled. I was a new man.

Don't exaggerate, Dan, Julia would shake her head, in the early days. You have been married after all! She worried I must still be grieving for Margaret. She would feel better, she said, in a way, if I had simply left my wife, or she me. A dead rival was so much more formidable than a living one. She would grow thoughtful and I would be obliged to find words for a past I had never properly examined: Margaret took charge of me, I eventually concluded, when I was young and inexperienced. Taught me sex in a bed, away from meadows and angry bullocks. Took me to the town hall and gave me a child almost before I grasped what was happening. My feelings for her were gratitude, dutifulness, awe. She guided my life, encouraged me to concentrate on my career. No need to waste time socialising, she would say. No need to have other friends. Ambitious for me in the early years, as time passed and our daughter grew up she became disappointed, wistful. I was always looking at other women, she said. Why had I come home late? Why had I started to pay so much attention to my personal appearance? I was perplexed. It worried me to see her unhappy. Do you want me to give an account of every minute of my day? I asked. If it makes you feel better, I will. And she said yes, please, every minute when you're not with me. So I did. I jotted down my movements for her, handed her the piece of paper when I came home. Left it on the kitchen counter, rather. You can call me any time, I said, when mobile phones arrived. I was completely faithful.

Julia rolled her eyes. She couldn't believe I had accepted such a demeaning arrangement. But I never felt it was demeaning, I explained. On the contrary, I had offered to do it, willingly. I wanted things to be okay between us.

Still Margaret wasn't happy: even Rachel could see, she told me, that I was looking at other women. All the time. Which other women, I asked. I was baffled. All of them, she said.

So the reason, I explained to Julia, that I applied for a live-in headship in a remote Yorkshire boarding school was to set my wife's mind at rest once and for all. If we both lived and worked in the same building, full time, how could she suspect me? We managed to arrange for Margaret to run the school infirmary. It was so much easier than hospital nursing. Rachel slept in the dormitory with other girls her age. She seemed happy enough.

Sometimes you frighten me, Julia said. You literally put yourself in prison for this woman. You must have loved her enormously.

Not *literally*, I laughed. *Practically.*

Did I love her? I was trying to solve a problem, to re-establish a quiet fruitful married life. And to prove my innocence. It worked. Margaret and I became an emblematic institutional couple. For five or six years. Pupils and staff looked up to us. We did our duty by the school, saved a lot of money. It wasn't a bad time.

Julia shook her head.

But then Margaret began to complain about the kind of people I was recruiting. They're all women, she said. This wasn't strictly true. But for every man applying for a post there were ten highly qualified women. That's school life these days. And always the same *kind* of woman, she insisted. I couldn't see it. Alison? Leah? Bernadette? An RE teacher from Trinidad, in her forties. A well-to-do London graduate for Accounts and Purchasing. A peppy Belfast maths teacher, immediately popular with all the kids. I couldn't remember a maths teacher being so popular. How could three women be more different? You're either stupider than I thought, Margaret decided, or more devious.

Julia smiled. Everyone knows that a man recruiting women chooses those who attract him. It's normal, isn't it?

But I didn't, I protested. There were five of us on the selection committee.

You do realise, Margaret said, that you never take your eyes off her at staff meetings. She meant Bernadette. You're always marvelling about how the kids love their maths teacher. It's embarrassing.

In my Zürich hotel I wash socks and underwear, shorts and shirt, in the sink. At least the heat guarantees they'll be dry before morning. Then head out, into the street, across the river and up to the old town. The truly huge clock on the cathedral tower tells me it's seven fifteen. It seems the Swiss lose all sense of proportion when it comes to time. And they love to crowd their shop windows with neat and colourful rows of things: cakes and chocolates; pipes and pocketknives; herb teas, jewels, jams. Each colourful item rigorously in line, neatly labelled, clearly priced. There's even a Condomeria, with condoms and vibrators in pink and purple rows, attractive and respectable as the Rolex and the Swarovski.

If it's not time for a ring yet, let me get you a necklace, I told Julia. For the evenings she had packed two light summer dresses, a blue and a red. And sandals. After almost five years, the pleasure I took in being beside her had only increased. It was the pleasure, I suppose, of discovering myself a quite different Daniel Burrow from the one who had done his duty by Margaret in a boarding school in north Yorkshire. As if I'd only now really arrived in life.

Not my wife maybe, I whispered, but my midwife!

I love it, she murmured, when you say these crazy things.

And I'm simply dying to buy you something.

But she didn't want gold or silver, or pearls, or pretty semi-precious stones. At a market stall by the river she chose bright clunky beads of bubble-gum pink.

Fantastic! she laughed, turning this way and that in the mirror a man held up for her.

I'm always a bit envious, I told her later, how women have the panache to wear such bright and beautiful stuff.

55

We were sitting at a table in a small square.

Oh, men can do it too, she said. Look at him!

On a column above an elaborate fountain, a bronze soldier was sporting a curly pointed beard and feathered cap. His shapely breastplate and white greaves seemed elegantly camp.

Go for it! she teased.

I'm looking at the same statue now. The brave soldier has a flag in one fist and a sword in the other, left foot lifted, ready to march. Traditionally, men dressed their smartest to fight, I suppose. As if only the risk of death could excuse such vanity. And though I can't see Julia's face, opposite me here, at my table in the square, I can see those pink beads we bought that evening, warm against the tan of her skin, the swell of her cleavage.

I order steak. The cobbles have soaked up the sun and are releasing the noontime heat into the evening air. Bernadette also wore bright beads the day she came to my office and declared her love. She was a tiny woman and the beads seemed huge on her birdlike pertness. Why did I never tell Julia this? I told her about falling into a heap of manure, and the time, diving into Lake Windermere on a school journey, my trunks slid down to my ankles; the children were delighted; but not about Bernadette Walsh's declaration of love.

Perhaps they were eggs, rather than beads. Painted birds' eggs. Is your wife poorly? the maths teacher asked one day in the corridor coming from the annexe. Margaret had given up working in the infirmary some time ago.

Children at private schools were spoiled and hypochondriac, she complained, their rich parents phobic and hypercritical. She had withdrawn from school life, retreated to our small flat up on the third floor, fallen prey to depression. You seem anxious, Headmaster, Bernadette told me. And perhaps a week later the Irish woman came to my office, wearing bright yellow birds' eggs strung round her neck, and said she could no longer hide the fact she was in love with me.

I didn't tell this to Julia, I reflect, gazing at the soldier on his column, and beneath him a couple of cyclists have stopped to fill their caps from the fountain and pour the water over their heads, because I felt ashamed. In a way I never felt remotely ashamed about manure heaps or swimming trunks. Miss Walsh, I said as neutrally as I could, I don't think this is the time or place.

I texted my shrink, Julia announced, about Catherine's message.

The evening was cool after the afternoon's rain and we had gone back to the hotel for our wind jackets, then come out again to drink a glass of wine on the waterfront where Lawrence had caught the steamer southbound to Kilchberg. In those days, Julia said, it was a regular commuter service from early morning to late evening. Now there were only a few tourist boats in the middle of the day; we planned to rise early and take the 'S'. Three stops.

And what did she say?

That I'm doing the right thing. Sophie as well, she added. Sophie was a friend. One of her confidants.

A brass band had begun to play, half a dozen young men swinging their instruments from side to side. The waterfront milled with tourists.

What if they said you were doing the wrong thing? I asked.

Julia laughed. They never would.

Julia had four or five confidants. Women and men. She told them all about us, discussed her quandaries back and forth. They were work colleagues or childhood friends. Sometimes we wined and dined with them. At their homes. In Richmond and Ealing. Or in restaurants we considered 'safe'. I no longer asked Julia if it wasn't inevitable, telling so many people, that the truth trickle through to Peter. Or her children. Was that what she wanted? I'd once asked. Not at all, she insisted. They were all people who could keep a secret. Rather she worried that I had no one to talk to. How can you hold it all in? she asked.

I let it hang out with you.

A person needed friends, she thought. A range of views. To stay balanced.

But yours always tell you you're doing the right thing!

Nothing had irked Margaret more than when I went out with old friends. In the days before we buried ourselves in Yorkshire. To play squash, perhaps. My friends were her enemies. Perhaps we'd have a pint afterwards. In Manchester this was, where I'd grown up. But then nor did I particularly enjoy sharing Julia with her friends. They were university people, secure in their views and values, not hiding their surprise that Julia was in love with a geography teacher of all things, and a headmaster, a figure of authority. Surely one went to a lover for an alternative sort of guy, they joked.

I'm happy to leave the school, I had told her. Time and again. I'll hand in my notice tomorrow, if it means we can be together. I had been growing concerned about Catherine. In her last year at the time, the girl was regularly contesting her teachers. She ignored the uniform rules, cropped her hair herself, ate next to nothing. A group had formed around her. She thrived on disruption. Whenever another pupil was disciplined, for whatever reason, she took their side, organised protests. Was I allowing things to get out of hand because the girl's mother was my lover?

I'm not too old to do something different, I said.

Julia was upset. You're a born headmaster, she told me. I don't want you to sacrifice yourself for me, like you did for Margaret. She kissed me hard.

So where's that woman of mine? Despairing of sleep in the stifling room with the window wide open on the din of the pub below, I recall the words I would have said, I always said, when I climbed into bed with Julia.

Where's my woman then? Where is she?

Your woman? Delusions of possession, eh, Mr Burrow?

Or I would say, Who's this woman in my bed?

And who are you to ask . . . ?

And so the tussle began till we fell asleep in each other's arms and towards dawn, that night in Zürich, and this is one of the things I remember with great clarity, I woke to find her shaking in the bed beside me, head twisting back and forth, tangled hair covering her face. No! she was shouting. No!

I shook her shoulder.

Dan! she cried.

I made tea. There was a kettle. A selection of Twinings bags. We sat up against the bedstead and I remember there was a mirror opposite, though I can't see our faces in it now. She had been on the flat roof of a department store, she explained. Somewhere in the West End. The sky was huge, there was a fabulous view of the city and, walking to the edge, you could look down into streets teeming with life. She had felt exhilarated, happy. Until she realised there was no way down. How had she got up there? She didn't know. There was just the flat cement roof with a sheer drop on all sides and the city all around. No way back into the store. She panicked, began to run this way and that. Then a dog appeared. From nowhere. Perhaps it had been there all along. It wasn't clear. It wasn't clear whether the dog was Bobbie, her collie, or not. It was wagging its tail. She had bent down to pat it and it stretched up to lick her face. They were friends. The dog has come to show me how to get down from the roof, she thought. Dogs can always find their way home. The creature backed off a little and barked at her. Yap yap yap. It was trying to say something. The more she didn't understand, the louder the creature barked. It snarled and bared its teeth. She felt distressed. Suddenly the dog turned and dashed straight over the edge of the roof. Feeling giddy, she stumbled after it. Far below, a crowd of people were gathering around something on the pavement. Now she was going to fall too. No! she shouted. No!

And pretty damn loud! I laughed.

She tried to smile. I feel bad for the dog.

Right. But rather him than you, no?

By this time dawn was breaking. We dressed and headed for the train station, a long day's walk ahead.

The pub is finally silent. I take another cold shower and slumber a little. Now I'm awake again. The thing with insomnia is to let it unfold, savour your thoughts, never be angry. Isn't it odd, for example, amid so much lost by the wayside, that I should remember this dream of hers? Or at least part of it. Perhaps she only told me part. I definitely remember her mentioning the department store. And me saying, Your love of shopping, huh?

A mosquito is whining. If I cover myself with the bedclothes I'll be too hot. If I don't, I'll be bitten. I remember my own dream yesterday. Margaret still alive, in a living-dead kind of way. Dreams give you back the past, perhaps, like cobbles breathing back heat. You don't seem upset at all, Rachel accused me, after the funeral. And it was true. I couldn't grieve. I've done you a drawing, she said, for your Christmas present. I remember Julia at the door to our hotel room examining the plasters on her collar bones before shouldering her pack. Then we slipped quietly downstairs, through the plush Reception and out into the street.

Three a.m. *All the picturesqueness of Zurich is nothing*, I read. *It is like a most ordinary, average, usual person in an old costume.* How odd was it, I wonder, that for our honeymoon, as we sometimes called it, we chose to follow a man who hated the country he was walking through? At six I'm down at the door dropping the key in the box, as instructed.

'A figment, a fabrication'

If you don't want to live with us, we don't want to see you again, ever.

This was the text Julia read on the 'S' to Kilchberg, a ten-minute ride along the western shore of the Zürichsee, the split-level carriage surprisingly crowded despite the early hour, everyone dressed for work. And it's crowded again this morning, so much so that I have to sit with my pack on my lap. There's a station called Sanatorium. An anonymous white cube on the hill to the right, the lake a grey ribbon to the left. People pushing to the doors to get off at Kilchberg. As on that morning.

Now, as then, I am coffee-less. We started our walk hungry, climbing through a suburban clutter above the lakeside town, here a furniture showroom, there an old art nouveau villa, men in orange dungarees emptying bins, the road twisting and turning, up over the autobahn, as far as the small settlement of Adliswil, on the far side of the river Sihl, where Lawrence spent the night and met some Italians practising a play for carnival. *Bearers of a new spirit, something strange and pure and slightly frightening.* I read the passage on the train. He felt sympathetic towards these people, who had been condemned, as he saw it, to economic exile; but the following day he couldn't bear to go back to them in his thoughts. Something about the group disturbed him. *I shrink involuntarily away.*

And I shake my head. Nowt so queer as folk, as Margaret liked to say. How did we handle Catherine's text that morning? We walked in silence. Julia held the map and seemed particularly intent on our route. For the first time I struggled to keep up. The cafés weren't open yet in Adliswil, or not on the road that we took, and she didn't want to wait or explore. Beyond another railway line a steep scarp rises fifteen hundred feet to Felsenegg. Without a word, she led the way.

Am I going to do the same now? I'm pretty hungry, but settle into a steady stride, thoughtful and empty-headed. A few twists of a narrow lane, a cable-car wire sagging overhead, a young man waiting for his dog to perform, poo bag in hand. Then the path branches off to the left, tunnelling steep and dark into a broadleaf wood. I remember her walking ahead, back bent to the slope, as though determined to show how much energy she had. I can see her pack and her boots and her bare calves. Ducking under low branches, brushing aside strands of spider web. I remember wondering, How much longer can she keep this up? Deep in the woods, with the smell of the woods and the gloom, and the cooler, fresher air. The trees quite different here from yesterday's. No neat rows. No stacks of timber. Trunks leaning this way and that. Mosses and dead leaves, acorns and ivies, everything dense and green, dewy and brown. The bark and the fallen twigs and the dark black earth. Already I'm breathing hard, sweating profusely. I need to stop. I need a stick perhaps. Up and up. Panting now. On and on. Until at last she went down. On a rock beside the path. She sat down and plunged her face in her hands. I wait until there is a bench, of kinds. A split trunk across a couple of stones. And sit beside her. Say nothing.

It's silent here. Not eight o'clock yet. Everything limp and cold. Hearts beating fast. It's quite a climb on an empty stomach. Her thick hair falling forward. Eventually she sighed and pulled out her phone. We exchanged glances. She bit her lip. Then she was pressing the keys. I waited, breathing deeply. She paused and we exchanged another glance. Half a smile. Then back to the phone, her fingers quick and wilful. Stabbing the keys. As if she could force her daughter to see reason, with the pressure and precision of her fingertips. How often had I watched Julia texting, slim fingers intent on persuading someone? Someone else-where. Occasionally glancing up at me. The hands falling still for a moment. Strong, pale fingers, a pale lacquer on the nails. And that wry, pained smile. I wanted this to end.

She sat a moment, holding the phone in her open palms, watching the screen, hoping for an immediate reply. A couple of minutes. Then got to her feet.

Sorry, Dan.

For heaven's sake.

My legs are stiff, after the break. I really should have packed some snacks. With the thick foliage there's no way of telling how much further you have to climb. But then stiffness is a pleasure in its way. And hunger. And not knowing how long you'll have to sweat. The pleasure of being *in it* all again. The path zigzags up the steep scarp. Back and forth across a dry stream. Here and there a little muddiness and a few flies. Roots clutching at the stones. I remember at one point we heard voices behind us, through the trees. Julia quickened her pace. She never liked to be overtaken. But then came a tinkle of laughter. A girl's. And a snatch of song. Quite close. Baritone. Julia stopped. No point in racing when you're beaten. She took my hand. The couple were young, with light shoes, small packs. They sped past, almost dancing up the steep path. Broad smiles on their faces. *Grüezi!* they called. Julia waited till the voices faded. If only Catherine had a boyfriend, she muttered.

There's no one else on the path this morning. I feel no haste or anxiety walking alone. Nothing can happen. It occurs to me that I was always a little anxious back then. Anxious that Julia would find the walking too much. As if it were my project, not hers. Or that I would let her down in some way: book a miserable hotel, calculate our walking times wrong. Perhaps it was part of being in love. I was anxious that we be happy.

The path skirts a cable-car pylon, then meets a narrow lane. One more steep climb, a couple of hundred yards, and you're out of it, on top, in Felsenegg. There are neatly mowed greenswards, a gently tilting plateau. At a crossroads a signpost bristles with destinations. Sendeturm. Stallikon. Pluto in Sonnenferne. But to our dismay the big café for the cable-car folk was closed. It wouldn't open till ten.

We crossed the terrace to the parapet. The view is

vast. Adliswil smokes directly below; roads criss-cross through a scatter of housing, then the roofs of Kilchberg and the long thin line of the lake like a streak of mercury. To the left the tower blocks of Zürich pick up bright sun-beams through fleecy cloud. *Laid out before me like a relief map*, Lawrence says. But to the right, on the far horizon beyond the lake . . .

The mountains! Julia cried.

It was our first view. The mountains were to be the real adventure of this trip. A jagged fairy-tale silhouette, rising behind blue hills. Delicate and magnificent. It seemed there was no connection between this world and that. Ordinariness here, extraordinariness there. Gazing together, arm in arm, our mood shifted. We cursed the tardy Swiss but refused to wait an hour for breakfast and set out at a brisk pace, south towards the Albis Pass.

This morning I gaze down from the same parapet and try to feel what Lawrence felt. *I could not believe*, he says, *that that was the real world. It was a figment, a fabrication, like a dull landscape painted on a wall*. Watching a train trundling along the shore, it looks real enough to me. Certainly an excellent vantage point for observing the various features of glaciation. Yet, as my eye ranges back and forth, over the wooded hills and pasture lands, the sprawl of Zürich and the smooth moraine spurs sliding into the glassy lake, I do experience an inkling of detachment, as if the panorama were no more than a painted model. You might be in a classroom, pointing to the blackboard. Everything is exemplary, everything is clear. At once I feel there must be something lurking behind that clarity. Something I'm not seeing and could never convey in any lesson. It's an odd thought.

Of course I knew the café would be closed. It's not even nine. Though I realise I'd been nursing half a hope they might have changed their opening hours. No such luck. The big building is deserted, brown chairs tipped up against neat rows of tables. At one corner a life-size plastic cow is red and white, like the Swiss flag. You can almost hear its plastic moo. The paths are neat here too. Narrow lanes rather. Smooth grey asphalt snaking across lush grass. The plateau is a nature park. The trees are tagged again. *Traubeneiche, Quercus petraea. 14b*. Abundant information boards explain the flora and fauna. In four languages. Sweet woodruff. Brown hare. Then the *Planetenweg*. Julia stopped to read: Would you like to reach for the stars? Every metre you cover from Felsenegg to Uetliberg represents one million of the 5.9 billion kilometres from Pluto to the Sun. Visit the planets by the side of the path along your way.

Space travel at last, she enthused.

The information was provided by the Zürich Astronomical Society.

We're headed the other way, I pointed out. On *Naturfreundeweg*.

She thumped two fists against my chest. Trust Mr Geography to bring me back to earth!

I laughed, put my arms round her. For a few moments we relaxed into each other, speechless beyond anxiety and banter. I distinctly remember that embrace, here in this very place, my head beside hers, looking over her shoulder at the information board that showed the orbits of the planets around the sun: Merkur, Venus, Erde, Mars, Ceres, Jupiter, Saturn. For perhaps a minute we were the centre of the universe, breathing gently together.

Naturfreundeweg passes by a golf course. Already I'm regretting the wild tangle of the wood. How unreal would Lawrence have found these manicured greens, the bunkers and the buggies? Beside the path a tree fungus looks like a white squid. Up ahead, the panorama flows away, oceanic, towards the distant reef of the Alps. After an hour or so, in one of the dips, between giant waves of meadowland, you come to the Albis Pass, and, at last, the Albis Café. *Seit 1957*. Again there's a terrace. Two men talking business with their computers open. A woman alone with the *Neue Zürcher Zeitung*. So, I asked Julia, what did you reply?

It's just after ten. The waiter is prompt and courteous. Speaks good English. The café crème is strong and the pastry he brings dense and sugary.

Just that I love her, she said.

It seemed to me she must have written more than that. But was there anything I could usefully say? We sat on the same side of the table and unfolded two maps, local and national. It was a moment of wellbeing, with the kick of the coffee and the thick nutty paste of the *Nussgipfel*. We looked at one map, then the other.

What if we speed things up a bit? she said.

Lawrence had walked through Baar to Zug, eight miles south of here. Then proceeded in a strangely roundabout fashion. First another eight miles down the east side of

Lake Zug, to Arth, where he spent the night. Then the following morning climbing Mount Rigi, four thousand feet, before scrambling down to the north-west, between Lake Zug and Lake Lucerne, picking up a tram to travel the last miles to Lucerne itself.

There was nothing important for her research, Julia said, in that part of the trip. We might as well catch a train to Lucerne from Zug. Saving a day. What mattered were the mountains, beyond Lake Lucerne. It was there Lawrence had made his important observations.

I went inside the restaurant to pee and pay. All I recall, looking out now from the same terrace across a bucolic valley where a tractor is turning cut grass in the bright sunshine, is how confused I felt. There was always a wonderful easiness in being with Julia, in the spaces we carved out for ourselves. Away from Julia I hardly existed. But the way forward, beyond those tight spaces, was never clear. This decision to shorten our trip had to do with her daughter's text. I was sure of that. We would cross the mountains, but instead of spending the summer in Italy as planned, she would hurry us back to London, to her children. We needed to discuss this.

The proprietor fussed with his credit card terminal. The connection was slow. When I returned to the terrace, Julia was leaning against the rail overlooking the car park, phone at her ear. Frowning. Then smiling. Shrugging. Tossing back her hair. Laughing. Every gesture a little exaggerated, a little false. She turned to make a face; I already knew she was speaking with her husband.

Peter called. She swung her pack onto her back.

About Catherine?

No. He didn't mention her.

So?

He just wanted to know how my research was going. It's like – she hesitated – he refuses to understand, you know, that I'm not coming back. How many times do I have to tell him?

Before we get going, I said, have we decided to cancel the booking in Arth? If so, I should phone the place.

From the Albis Pass, we dropped down to a small lake, Türlersee. There are bulrushes and marshy grasses. It's easy walking, but the path is narrow, you risk getting your feet wet, so we were in single file again. Me in front now, crossing a narrow wooden bridge. Julia was flagging. At the same time, sensing my uneasiness, she kept trying to cheer me up, calling to look at this or that: wild strawberries in the grass, the tracks of some small animal, a church spire in the distance; the inevitable clock. It was midday already.

We climbed through some farmland and at the top of a field found the way barred by an electric fence. You had to take off your pack, get down on the grass, and roll underneath.

Lower, I warned. I put my hand gently on her hair.

She turned her face up from the ground, below the fence, with a wry grin. Come here, Dan. She reached a hand. I got down and we lay together in the grass, inches from the blue wire, cheek to cheek, looking at the sky.

I'd love to make love, she whispered.

That might be tricky.

We lay there a few moments, each thinking our own thoughts, before I told her, You know, at Grubenhof, one of my jobs was to check the electric fence. Every morning, before driving the cows to the field.

And how do you do that?

By giving yourself a shock.

You're joking!

There's a trick. You pick a long stalk of grass, hold one end in your fingertips and let the other touch the wire. If the electricity is on, you get a sharp kick in your wrist and elbow. Like you'd fired a gun.

You poor love! You must have hated it!

I knew she would enjoy this story.

But actually I didn't hate it. I remember now how strange it felt, trudging alone up the hill above the farm to whatever field the herd would be spending the day in. I would switch on the alternator and listen to its slow tick. But a circuit like this is easily broken, by a passing animal, or even a bramble, dew laden, pressing against the wire somewhere. So it has to be tested. I found my stalk of grass and pulled my hand into the sleeve of my work jacket so I could hold it through the coarse material. Then I looked at the wire for a few seconds, preparing myself. When I was ready, I lowered the end of the stalk to touch it. Wham! The current shot into my arm. It was unpleasant and unsettling. But very intense. I always felt oddly pleased with myself.

Julia rubbed her cheek against mine. You frighten me, Dan Burrow, she said.

We frighten each other, I told her.

71

She sighed. The blue wire above our eyes seemed to fuse with the sky.

In a soft voice, she said, Cathy's message changes nothing, Dan. I'm only eager to get to the mountains. Eager for life to begin.

We kissed, taking great care.

Electrifying, she murmured.

Walking towards Baar, along narrow tracks through tidy farmland, barns and stacked hay and tall stands of maize, I think about Catherine. About the last two occasions I saw her, just a few weeks before she would be sitting her A levels. The final-year 'A' stream had declared a strike. A boy had been expelled and they were protesting. What will your parents think, I asked, as I stood in front of the class, if you jeopardise your careers like this?

They sat mute, braced for conflict, eager to be adult.

You, Elaine, I admire your loyalty to your classmate, but what do you hope to achieve by this? Really?

Elaine was a cheerful, diligent girl. I guessed she was dying to drop the whole thing and get back to normal.

Rules are rules, I went on.

Nothing.

Okay, if Elaine doesn't want to speak, what about Pankaj? Let's hear your take on all this.

In the front row, the boy hesitated. A bright, sporty kid. Well, sir—

You're destroying someone's life! Catherine interrupted. She sat to one side of the class, leaning against the wall.

Pankaj?

He looked at his hands. Let Cathy say it.

Okay, I said. I didn't ask her, but go ahead, Catherine.

To look at she would have been a youthful version of her mother, if only she had eaten properly. But her cheeks were hollow, her hair roughly chopped in reddish tufts. Nevertheless, the look gave her a kind of authority, as if she were more real than the more conventional girls, more earnest. She spoke with intensity, unafraid of eye contact. All this is hypocrisy, she said. Everybody smokes dope. Who cares?

The others murmured.

My mum smokes dope! And she's a university professor.

Everybody laughed.

Probably you do too, she added. Sir.

I smiled and turned my eyes to the class. As I'm sure you know, Ryan has not been expelled for smoking marijuana, but for selling it. On school premises. Along with other drugs. Two pupils who bought from him have only been reprimanded.

There are no sellers without buyers, Catherine shot back. If people like my mother, like you, didn't buy drugs, no one would sell them.

It is important never to seem uneasy in front of a class of adolescents. But her speaking of her mother and myself in the same breath was disquieting.

For the record, Catherine, I do not buy drugs. Or consume them. Again I turned my eyes to the others, as if to let her know her time was up. She had had her say.

I said people *like* you, she came back, undeterred. *For*

the record. For sure she was sharp. As was her mother, for that matter.

Kids, let's stay focused on what has happened. It is a crime to sell marijuana and indeed amphetamines. Ryan was committing a crime, in school. We had no choice but to expel him.

Pankaj raised his hand. Sir, we were just hoping he could have another chance. Maybe after a short suspension.

There was a murmur of assent.

Thank you, Pankaj. I know Ryan is popular. I appreciate your spirit of solidarity. I am sure he will have another chance, but not at this school. Without this punishment, it will be hard for him to grasp the seriousness of what he has done.

All the time I was speaking I was aware of the girl's eyes on me, aware that if the plans that Julia and I were making came to fruition, she would become my step-daughter. Was I treating her the way I would treat another pupil who spoke to me like this?

Let me add one last thing, I wound up. It is honourable to want to defend others, but Ryan is perfectly able to speak for himself and has spoken for himself. He has admitted what he did and accepted that we were obliged to inform the police. Why should you harm yourselves on his behalf?

A small chapel appeared, to our left, alone on the green hillside, with a little veranda in front and a low hedge all around. The roof is strangely pagoda-like, with red tiles, then a green copper tower, topped with a little dome and an iron cross. An odd amalgam of styles. We followed a path beside a fence to take a look. The door was locked, but on the wall under the roof there is a fresco of men in armour, sitting jollily together, helping themselves from a big bowl of some white liquid. *Milchsuppe zu Kappel 1529*, runs a legend in Gothic script. I muddled through an explanatory plaque, in German: a battle between Catholic and Protestant armies had been avoided at the last minute and the soldiers who were to fight fraternised and drank milk soup together.

Good omen, Julia laughed.

Except then they did fight – I read the bottom lines of the plaque – two years later, almost in this same spot. Thousands slain.

You seem determined to exasperate us all, I told Catherine. Her maths teacher had sent her to my office.

She was silent.

Mr Robb says you have been making inappropriate gestures.

I blew him a kiss, she said. Like this . . . She pouted and kissed her fingertips. I remember her hands seemed chapped.

From what he reported, it appears there was rather more than that.

She was silent.

Just another couple of weeks, Catherine, I said, and the torment of school will be over. It might be an idea to concentrate on your exams.

She kept shifting position on her seat, looking round the room, my office, scratching the inside of a wrist. But then her eyes would find and hold my gaze, even raising an ironic eyebrow. Exactly as her mother did.

You've applied for university, am I correct? I'm told you have a couple of excellent offers. Things are looking good.

I won't be going to university, she said.

These two encounters, the one only a couple of days after the other, created a dilemma I hadn't foreseen. The natural thing would have been to tell Julia. But there was the danger that, alarmed by what the girl had done and said, her mother would start quizzing her and Catherine would understand that we were in contact. Of course, I could ask my secretary to inform her officially, which would put Julia in a position to confront her daughter, but that seemed rather heavy, given the friendly, smoothing-over approach I had been taking. It made no sense to alienate the poor girl if we were to be family. There was nothing drastic in what she'd done. On the other hand, if I didn't tell Julia but then Catherine did, she might feel upset I hadn't mentioned it. I remember worrying about this for a day or two, then three or four, until the decision was, in a way, already taken, since Julia and I had seen each other once, then twice – her book-club evenings – without my having said anything. But the following week, grabbing a coffee together, she told me Cathy had been telling her some disturbing stories about her maths teacher, that he was after one of the girls in her class. She hadn't been sure whether to refer this to me but in the end decided she should. It sounded like grooming, she thought.

The little town of Baar was as nondescript as they come,

and Zug, two miles on, only a little better. We were tired. It was after two. On the train I admitted I was disappointed that we weren't sticking to Lawrence's exact route. She said she had had a couple of ideas that she absolutely must write up this evening. She leaned across the seats and took my face in her hands. Don't go obsessive on me, Dan. Nobody in the literary world gives a damn whether I actually go everywhere Lawrence did. The important thing is that we have a good time.

The ticket machine in the foyer of Zug station offers all kinds of options that I can't rightly understand. It's only a fifteen-minute ride to Lucerne. A poster outside the Migros supermarket shows two moustached men in Swiss-red T-shirts, mouths approaching for a kiss, while one holds a chocolate-coated ice cream at a suggestive angle. *Einfach gut leben*, says the caption. Julia had pointed out to me, I remember, that all the people Lawrence describes meeting and befriending along his walk were young men. He was known to have homosexual leanings, and she wondered if that was why he had left Frieda behind and made the trip alone. We bought bread and cheese and apples in Migros and ate a late lunch on the train. Peter would probably find it easier to understand that you really are leaving, I told her, if you made it clear you were with someone.

Soon now, she said.

'Like the wrapper round milk chocolate'

Hotel Schlüssel was more expensive than we would have wished. I remember the place for its unusual name – Key Hotel, I told Julia – and when Google Maps leads me there sure enough a lock turns and I catch a fleeting glimpse of two weary figures with blue backpacks pushing through wood-panelled doors. There was a small queue before us at Reception and the garrulous proprietor, in his seventies, was offering lengthy and identical explanations to each and every customer regarding breakfast arrangements and internet access and check-out requirements. Yes of course he could book a steamer and cable-car package, he told the couple immediately in front of us. But do you really want to go tomorrow when the weather is expected to be poor? How far ahead do I need to book? the man fussed. He was tall, with swept-back white hair, possibly American, shabby and moneyed, constantly turning to his partner for confirmation, which she, in a flowery blouse and loose linen trousers, invariably gave, nodding and smiling reassuringly.

Why do I remember this trivial scene so clearly when so much else is forgotten? Standing in line on a plush red carpet, I could not believe the old proprietor was once again going to start explaining that breakfast was served from six thirty to ten and that your plastic key must be inserted in the appropriate slot inside the door to turn on the electricity in the rooms. Julia rolled her eyes. Now the American was asking which of three possible round trips offered the best value for money. And how do you suggest we dress? Eventually, his partner raised herself on tiptoe and pulled his ear towards her mouth. He turned, saw us and made an expansive gesture, opening his arms wide, walking stick in one hand. Oh I am so sorry, you folks! Please do go ahead and check in. My, but you look tired! What have you been up to?

So it was that hours later, as we stepped into the hotel restaurant, the same man, now in a green corduroy jacket with loose blue necktie, once again opened his arms, this time to call us to his table, as if we somehow owed it to him to be his guest. Julia glanced at me, I assented. Why not? Asking for wine, he began to tell us about his work as a journalist. You might have seen my name, perhaps, Edwin Myers. He had covered the transition in Hong Kong. And the Arab Spring. In the pages of the *Herald Tribune*. His mother had been a personal friend of Giscard d'Estaing. The city of London, he assured us, occasionally letting his eyelids droop for a few seconds as he spoke, was the money-laundering centre of the world. Ongoing legacy of imperialism. Beyond disgrace.

His eyebrows were commandingly bushy. Likewise a thick white beard. The whole face expressed vigorous old age. Walking and yoga, he was saying now, were the only activities that kept body and mind in some kind of useful relationship. At my age, I mean. His daughter, of whom he was immensely proud, played viola for the Boston Philharmonic. By an earlier marriage, he clarified. Though without Barbara – he threw a proprietorial arm round the shoulders of the woman beside him – he would definitely have met with an early grave, or be chained, which was probably worse, to some institutional bed, in a straitjacket to boot. Again he closed his eyes, as though needing to dig deep to say these things. Apparently enjoying herself, Barbara nodded throughout, but with a wry, faintly detached smile, throwing in a He-really-did-you-know, from time to time, or a Yes-can-you-imagine? while the waiter came and went with shiny plates of hors d'oeuvres and cold cuts.

I settled down to watch Julia. She was always animated and engaging in company, leaning forward a little, bright eyes conveying encouragement and respect. I remember a sort of rosy dimness in the busy room, her freshly washed hair no doubt brushed over her left shoulder, and the feeling, almost at once, that all the energy at the table was coursing between her and Myers. He had written a book, he was saying, predicting American failure in Nicaragua; naturally the critics had trashed it, until every word came true. Then the publishers had rushed out a new edition, long after it was game, set and match to the Sandinistas.

Eventually Barbara found space to ask us how long we were staying in Lucerne and so Julia began to explain about our walk and her research. It was a question, she told them, of mapping the birth of modern eco-awareness in literature: the controlling psyche and the wounded planet. I had heard Julia speak at a couple of conferences in London and she was adept at implying a political slant to her studies that I never sensed when she talked to me. My impression was that she didn't rightly know why she was so fascinated by Lawrence. He was quite fearless, I remember her musing once, when it came to taking what he wanted, Frieda first and foremost. My grandmother, Edwin Myers was now commenting, was intimate with Dorothy Brett, you know, back in the thirties. The painter. New Mexico and so on. And she, Dorothy, had confided that Lawrence was impotent. Hundred per cent. My grand-mamma was quite a star, by the way, he added. Music hall. I had no idea who Dorothy Brett was. Julia quoted an authoritative work on the writer's sexuality and ongoing lung problems. Yale University Press. The two tossed ideas back and forth – Hadn't Lawrence set back the cause of feminism for decades? To the contrary, he had accelerated emancipation by igniting a fierce polemic. What mattered, Julia insisted, was to put difficult truths in the spotlight.

Sipping my wine, I noticed Barbara, diagonally across the table, shooting me occasional glances, one corner of her mouth creased in a smile that was almost mischievous. She must have been twenty years younger than him. At which I suddenly found myself wading into the conversation to say that whatever his health problems Lawrence was certainly an extraordinary walker. Covering thirty and more miles some days. Mountain miles at that. Fingers thrust in his hair, Edwin suggested that dear Bert – he smiled as he used the name – must have been exaggerating, no? Had anyone bothered to verify his movements? Why would he do that? I demanded. It was hardly a race. Edwin burst out laughing and again allowed his eyelids to droop and close. It was strange the effect this had, as if obliging you to contemplate the older man's triumph while forestalling any attempt to answer back. Julia remarked that actually, yes, an American scholar in the 1950s had produced an hour-by-hour timeline of Lawrence's progress from the moment he left Frieda until their reunion in Milan. But that was hardly the point; Lawrence never mentioned distances in the pages that he later wrote about the walk. He was only interested in the world he found, above all the way industrial uniformity was encroaching on rural culture. You bet it was, Edwin cried.

Barbara was smiling at me again. A pale, faintly sardonic smile. Are you a journalist too? I asked her. My Babs? Edwin pulled the woman close to him. Barbara's not a pundit, are you, love? She's a guru! I teach yoga, she said quietly, and meditation. For the first time there was a silence around the table, as if this calm, low voice, English to his American, required everyone present to press a reset button. Julia's daughter, I offered, is living in a meditation centre. Ah, Edwin exulted, I guessed you weren't a first marriage! Too happy by half! Barbara asked where. Julia explained that her daughter had simply wished to take some time off, do some growing up, before university, in search of a centre of gravity, as it were. She wasn't exactly living at this meditation place, but spending a month or so there, then a week at home. The other woman listened carefully and again asked what centre it was, which

tradition did it follow. So many of these outfits are run by
con men and megalomaniacs, Edwin opined. If not out-
right criminals. When Julia named the centre, in South
Wales, Barbara made no comment. Or did her eyes cloud
a little? Perhaps, she said, if Catherine should wish to
pursue this path, she might consider going abroad, to
Thailand for example. There were some excellent centres
there. I'm hoping she'll go to university, Julia laughed. Of
course, Barbara said, but she produced a card and passed
it over the tabletop: Psychoanalysis and Meditation (Thera-
vada Tradition). Edwin had written a novel, he started to
explain, oh years ago now, that revolved around an Indian
ashram being used as cover for an international corporate
conspiracy to brainwash the children of the world's elite
in view of a global power grab. I can't tell you, he confided,
with drooping eyelids, how frightened I made myself writing that book. Because as I did so I knew, simply knew,
that somewhere out there in this crazy world of ours it
must be happening. A major US publisher, he said, had
offered a six-figure sum for the novel, on condition that he
make certain, um, let's say, politically correct changes. I
refused, of course. He sat back, eyes closed for a moment,
mottled hands spread thumb to thumb on the tablecloth
as if in invitation to a séance. He really did, Barbara smiled.

In bed we chuckled until late. My father knew the Dalai
Llama, you know, who assured him the Buddha was gay.
My great-uncle on my mother's side ran a brothel in Rome
where Mussolini and the Pope discussed world domina-
tion. How did Barbara put up with the man? And the food
in his beard! To his credit, Julia acknowledged, he did

know about Dorothy Brett and Lawrence's New Mexico project. We lay pondering over the strange couple for some time, and likewise the strangeness and pleasure of meeting new people together, watching each other adapt and respond.

You're so smart, though, Julia thought, never saying much about yourself. I always get drawn in. I can't help it.

No one asked me, I said.

You don't encourage them. You don't need their interest. I love that in you. It's such a strength.

And I love the way you shine, I said. How animated you are.

We embraced. It really was a lovely room, as I recall, in the Hotel Schlüssel. With fresh linen sheets and mountains of plump pillows. Floral wallpaper. Bright mirrors. The more you told him what was what, I whispered, the more I was dying to get my hands on you.

How long, I asked a little later, has Catherine been going to that meditation centre?

Maybe eighteen months.

Barbara didn't seem impressed.

No.

We were holding hands, fingers caressing fingers in the dark. Then Julia said: Fact is, she eats when she's at the centre. They have a strict no-fasting rule. At home she won't touch a thing.

Lucerne and its lake were as irritating as ever—like the wrapper round milk chocolate. How consistent Lawrence is, I smile,

84

in his contrariness. Eating fish and chips in the Mr Pickwick Pub, I have smoothed out those pages, torn from a
Penguin paperback so many years ago. And I realise I'm
growing fond of the man, even when I don't agree with
him. I've been exploring the old town, crossing and re-
crossing the quaint covered bridge with the river sliding
silently beneath and the lake opening up to the right, silvery in the twilight. To me it seems charming. But then I'm
no enemy of milk chocolate either. Lawrence draws you
into an argument, I remember Julia saying. That's how he
hooks you. An argument about what, though? I wonder.
The fish and chips are surprisingly good in the Pickwick
Pub. He had hateful opinions on power relations between
men and women, Julia thought. But they were always
challenging, there was something serious to fight against. A
plaque on the wall tells me Charles Dickens also passed
through Lucerne. In 1853. I have no desire to fight with
anyone. Certainly I never fought Margaret. Was that our
problem? That we never shouted at each other? Never
really said the things that needed saying? Peter and I neither fight nor make up, Julia confided in one early conversation. She would have loved a good argument. It drove
her crazy. Her analyst had declared him confrontation-
averse. The only person spoiling for a fight, Julia said, is
Catherine. And I have no quarrel with her.

Someone is asking to share my table. I like this German
custom. Two young women. We don't speak to each other,
but I'm glad to hear their local dialect and to pick up a faint
perfume. I turn back to Lawrence and his quarrel with
Lucerne. *I could not sleep even one night there*, he says. *I took*

the steamer down the lake, to the very last station. There I found
a good German inn, and was happy.

We had decided to take the same steamer, but on the following morning, towards midday. That would allow us to
sleep late and take a wander round the town, then walk just
a couple of miles in the late afternoon. It's a three-hour trip
to the end of the lake. Julia had a blister she wanted to
rest. But now my table companions are getting excited
about something. I'm not sure what. They speak so
fast. Clearly they're close friends. Both blonde. They smile
brightly, shake their heads. A shrill laugh. Blue eyes plead.
One catches the other's wrist across the table. But equally
clearly they're arguing. Urgent protests from twisted lips. I
mustn't turn to look. Is it about a man? I can't be sure. For
some weeks I kept an eye on Catherine's maths teacher and
the friend he was supposedly grooming, but could find
nothing amiss. The girl seemed at ease and concluded her
school career that term with excellent results. I had never
heard anything but praise for him and it was hard to see
how I could ask any direct questions unless someone lodged
an official complaint. Had Catherine made the story up, I
began to wonder, in response to his having reported her
behaviour to me? Did she sense that her mother had a direct
line of communication with me? Was this a way of finding
out if that was the case? In all my school life I remember
only two teacher–pupil relationships that came to light. Mrs
Hargreaves, in Yorkshire, with a fifteen-year-old boy. She
was in her forties and they actually sent her down. It was
upsetting. I couldn't understand how she could have made

such an error of judgement. Then a younger fellow, Tim Hardy, with a sixth-form girl. That was some years later. Fortunately she had passed her eighteenth birthday, or had when they were discovered. Tim agreed to leave the school and later invited me to their wedding, though it would have been folly to go. No need to be anxious, Julia whispered when we kissed the first time. Only our second meeting, I think. In her Audi hatchback. It was she who moved her face to mine. Then asked for a pause for thought. A month at least, she said. I was craving for her. I had never experienced anything like it. We both know this can't lead to anything serious, she wrote next morning in a long email examining our situation. We were in bed within the week. The woman beside me has tears in her eyes now and is biting a lip. *Nein*, she says, *nein, das kann ich nicht.*

I'm not staying in the Schlüssel tonight. I've taken a cheaper place beyond the railway station. Shared bathroom across the corridor. When I try to turn on the light beside the sink, the electricity goes off with a pop. Thank God phones have torches these days. The man from Reception arrives with a roll of red insulating tape and unscrews the switch cover.

Laying my head on the pillow, the faces of the two women in the Mr Pickwick are very present to me. Their raised voices. A blue silk blouse. Neither of them wore their hair in a tress, or swept back across a shoulder. The tabletop where their fingers twined is turbulent as the waters jostling to Rhine Falls. The climb to Felsenegg was the best part of the day. That thick tangle of oak and undergrowth, following her bare calves up the steep slope. And the moment when she answered Myers quite sharply and told him difficult truths must be spoken. Barbara trying to signal something to me from a great distance. Thankfully, it's a dreamless night.

'So cruelly tired, so perishingly triumphant'

After three days of rising at dawn it was fun to order breakfast in bed. The tray arrived at nine with warm milk and coffee and croissants and fruit and fresh bread and cheese. Julia still hadn't turned on her phone. It seemed a positive development. We would soon be in the mountains.

To kill time before the steamer leaves, I ask in Reception if there's anywhere one can swim in the lake. But outside the weather has changed. The heat has gone from the air. A breeze is blowing. For the first time our weathers, past and present, coincide. It had been cool that morning at the Schlüssel, I remember.

Nevertheless any number of parents and children are splashing about in the shallow water at the beach. I swim out to the limit of the bathing area. Sails are scudding on the open water; there are big white motor yachts. Grey peaks rise into cloud. It's too bad we didn't find time to come here together back then. I loved swimming with Julia. I loved the powerful softness of her body, her slow breaststroke. She would tie her hair up to keep it dry, exposing a dark mole at the top of her neck. I remember her puffing out her cheeks as she breathed.

Of course, it occurs to me, drying off on a bench, if she had told Peter about us as soon as our affair got serious, she could have had all the arguments she wanted. But common sense dictated she mustn't do that while the children were at my school. My feeling was always that her family was her concern, that it would be a mistake to get involved. On the other hand, my happiness was in her hands.

There was quite a crowd at the quay and we had rushed to find a good place on the upper deck of the SS *Schiller*. The horn sounded to warn off the smaller boats, the paddles began to beat. Beyond the harbour the breeze picked up and the temperature dropped. A thin drizzle fell on spires and villas and hills. We pulled up our hoods. Then the ticket inspector came and told us our tickets were second class. The top deck was first class only. We could upgrade, I suggested. But Julia didn't want to. Julia was happy to spend, extravagantly at times, you could see she was used to having money, Peter was wealthy, but she hated feeling tricked. On the lower deck we squeezed onto a packed bench close to the port paddle which was throwing up clouds of spray.

There's no rain today, but the air is chill and damp. The steamer plies its way east along the north shore of the lake to Weggis and Vitznau. On a rocky promontory the stone figure of a monk has his arms outspread. Narrow branches of water open up to north and south, oddly luminous under heavy cloud. At Vitznau, where the cable car climbs to Rigi, there's quite a turnover. People are in a holiday mood despite the poor weather. Much laughing and shouting amid the spray from the paddle. I remember we ate rolls and blue cheese left over from breakfast. She always felt she was stealing a march, Julia said, when she could take away useful food from a hotel breakfast. Today I munch a supermarket sandwich watching two lively Asian women sharing beers with a Swiss man. They are on the bench in front of his but have turned round to chat. He is older than they are, speaking excitedly, gesturing, his sparse white hair hatless, cheeks ruddy. Peels of laughter. Selfies. Now they are exchanging phone numbers. I wonder how I would react if they turned to me.

For a while the shore is one grand hotel after another. Pink and cream palaces under steep woodland. Coloured domes, grey cliffs. Then at Gersau the boat empties before turning south on the last long branch of the lake to Flüelen. Julia pointed out a tall rock on the western shore. Even from this distance you can read the inscription. DEM SAENGER TELLS. F. SCHILLER. I wonder if Lawrence noticed it. He says nothing about the crossing in his book.

In my memory, too, this part of the trip is something of a lapse, or suspension. I remember our silent togetherness, cheek to cheek for warmth as the steamer turned into a stiff breeze. And a feeling of being transported towards a world ever more rugged and remote. Occasionally the clouds open, allowing a glimpse of dizzying crags, the bright thread of a waterfall, then the sky comes down again, low and grey.

Suddenly I'm bored and head to the cabin for a tea. There's hardly anyone around now. Flüelen isn't a popular destination it seems. In the central area of the steamer, beneath the bridge, they have exposed the boat's engine under a Perspex window. For the tourists' curiosity. The casing is a bright, plaything red: GEBRÜDER SULZER, WINTERTUR, 1906. You can stare at shiny steel pistons sliding back and forth. On the wall to one side, two rows of photographs show all the ship's captains since its launch. Ferdinand Schorno (1912–1932) sports splendid handlebar moustaches. Judging from Lawrence's descriptions of Swiss innkeepers, the style was in vogue. Kuno Stein (1990–2009) has designer glasses and a thick black beard. I don't recall our seeing him in the flesh. As of 2021 the SS Schiller has its first woman captain, Rebecca Benz. Julia would have been pleased, although looking closely at the cropped hair and steely features, it doesn't feel like much has changed.

The tea is scalding. I sit with my face in the steam, eyes closed. I hadn't realised how cold I'd got. The few people around are eager to be on the move; there's an end-of-journey impatience in the air. Outside you can see windsurfers streaking back and forth across the choppy water. The narrowing valley must channel the wind. Two in particular are trying to keep up with the steamer, a red sail and a blue. Man and woman, I think. But the wind is against them. They zip this way and that, forcing their boards round in a battle with the elements. And perhaps with each other. Do they want to be admired? Quite a few passengers are watching. Eventually, red sail hits a whitecap and flips. In a moment he's far behind, floundering in the waves. Blue turns back to help out.

I'm going to take a pee, I told Julia, before we arrive.

Good idea, she thought.

We both headed for the bathrooms, which were pleasantly warm. I washed my hands in hot water, then waited for her by a door with DAMEN written in Gothic script. Behind me the great engine cranked and throbbed, as it has for a hundred years. To one side there is a small window in the paddle casing. You can peer through and watch the big wheel churning in a white froth.

Dan?

I turned and Julia too was quite white.

I feel sick, Dan.

She held up her phone.

We know who you're with, the message said. Peter is destroyed. You've got to come back now.

A yellow crane stands beside the dock in Flüelen. Away from the beating of the paddles you notice a steady background noise. Above the eastern shore of the lake a fast road is cut into the mountainside. It half-circles the town to meet the autobahn that emerges from under the mountains at the bottom of the western shore. Heavy traffic flows southbound to Milan, northbound to Frankfurt. There are railway sidings, the clamour of a building site. Leaving the waterfront, we climbed a flight of cement steps through shabby housing, then picked our way among puddles in a dank tunnel under the road. So much for the world of mist and snow conjured up on the steamer.

It was in Flüelen that Lawrence had what Julia thought his most important encounter of the trip. In the dining room of his hotel a red-faced Englishman was dunking bread into warm milk. Uneasy at first, wanting only to be alone, this young man eventually told his story. With no knowledge of German, no previous experience of the mountains and very little money, he had travelled from London to Switzerland, walked the high ridges of the Rhône and Furka glaciers, covering more than a hundred miles in four days, and now, his short holiday over, was heading home with a strict schedule of steamers and trains to get him back behind his office desk for Monday morning. *He was so cruelly tired, so perishingly triumphant*, Lawrence wrote.

Leaving Flüelen for the short walk south to Altdorf, a Burger King logo on a high mast is visible for miles. We chose a longer route than necessary to get above the ribbon development on the floor of the valley. There are drystone walls up here, streams and pastureland, but the roar of the autobahn persists and the realisation that it would be with us for much of our walk to Italy added to our mood of dejection. A thin drizzle was sifting down.

Julia quickened her step. She wanted to reach our hotel and have somewhere to sit down and take stock. So I supposed. But now, some way ahead, she stopped. Like so many paths in Switzerland, this one had occasional wayside games or curiosities for children. Here a shiny black tube about four feet tall rose vertically from the grass beside a bank of holly. Say something! Julia called. It was a speaking tube. She was standing by its partner twenty yards ahead; apparently the two were connected underground.

I bent down. The mouthpiece was the height of a five-year-old. Julia had her ear to the other. I love you, I whispered. All will be well.

I remember standing up, to see if she had heard. She was already turning her mouth to the tube. Pressing my ear to the opening, I was aware of a peculiar hollowness. I waited. It wasn't exactly silence, more as if someone had made a noise long ago, the faintest echo of which was trapped underground. Then her voice came through with a metallic ring: I'm so scared, Dan.

Altdorf is the town where William Tell refused to show obeisance to the foreign tyrant, Hermann Gessler, as a result of which he was set the task of shooting the apple off his son's head. In 1307. You can't get away from this story here. There is the Wilhelm Tell Pizzeria, the Tellen-bräu restaurant, the Tellsgasse, the Tellskapelle, the Tell-denkmal. Our hotel was just a stone's throw from the square where it happened. In our room I found a kettle and the inevitable Twinings bags. Julia sipped Earl Grey and stared out of the window.

You know, maybe it's for the best, I said. You won't have to tell them now, will you? It's done.

She didn't reply.

After a while I asked, Does she always call her father Peter?

Yes.

And you Julia?

Jewel, she said. Peter's name for me.

She stood by the window, cradling her cup, swaying from side to side. I had never called her Jewel.

Why not phone now? I said. Or better still, phone Peter. Get it over with.

She sighed, bit a lip. I wonder if there's a hairdryer here, she said. She went to look in the bathroom. I could hear cupboards opening. Drawers. What if it's a bluff, Dan? she called. What if it's a bluff and she doesn't know anything at all?

I hadn't thought of this.

Coming back, Julia slumped in an armchair, put her face in her hands and began to cry. I sat on the end of the bed. Her shoulders trembled. I remember thinking that all this was unnecessary, stupid even. At the same time crying always moves me.

Eventually she pushed her hair back and wiped her eyes on a sleeve.

I wanted to tell them myself, she said. Not to be caught out.

We showered and went to find a restaurant. The rain was falling more steadily. On his plinth in the square, a tall bronze Tell has his hood pulled up against the cold, his crossbow slung over his shoulder. In skirts beside him, his boy looks like a curly-headed little girl.

At least we don't have to risk killing anyone, I said.

Give me a break, Julia muttered.

We chose our restaurant badly. It was too formal, too slow. The food too stodgy, the wine a little sour. The whole evening had a sour, slow, stodgy feel.

She didn't answer when I tried to call yesterday, Julia said. I'm not sure she wants to speak.

If Peter was really so upset, I suggested, he'd call you, wouldn't he?

She wasn't sure. Peter's a strange man, she said. All at once she started talking about Lawrence. The point about this Englishman he meets, she began, is that he thinks that in taking a holiday in the mountains he's enjoying some kind of freedom. But all his hiking is so wilful. He only has a few days and he treats the whole thing as a kind of monstrous task. Presumably to buoy up his self-esteem. And the reason he pushes himself so hard, walks so far and so fast, without taking time to enjoy himself, is precisely to repress the awareness that he's not free at all. The holiday is part of the larger machine he's trapped in. Meantime the people in the mountains adapt to accommodate this new kind of traveller who isn't really present except as an economic fact, here today gone tomorrow. They don't bother communicating about anything but services and prices.

I let her talk. I wondered if she was trying to tell me that she wouldn't be like the Englishman who just hurried out here then hurried home. I thought how much more at ease we would have been had she come clean with her family before leaving. But of course to tell the family about me barely a fortnight after her son left school would amount to confessing that she had been hiding things from them for ages. In the end I had no idea what the relationship between her and her children was. Or her and her husband. How could I? In all our four years together it had never come out that her daughter called her parents by their first names. Which seemed strange to me. And of course she *had* told them she was leaving home, she wanted a separation. What mattered, I decided, was the love I felt coming from her to me, and again from me to her. I had never felt surer about anything in my life.

It's a vicious circle, you see, she concluded: the man's determination is actually his enemy. Because deep down it's subjugated to this alienating zeitgeist.

I get all that, I said, but I wonder what Lawrence thought the alternative was. What should people be doing?

The first step is to become conscious of the situation, Julia said.

And then?

People should break out and live more freely.

I must have walked up and down the main street of Altdorf three or four times already. Looking for somewhere to eat. I don't like this place. I don't want to repeat our experience of years ago. The street itself is pretty enough. All the old buildings have been prettily renovated. The church has a charming red onion dome. But the flag of Canton Uri is everywhere: a black bull's head on a bright yellow background. The bull has a red ring in its nose and a bright red tongue that sticks out into the ring. It's disquieting and somehow makes all the prettiness disquieting too. I remember at Grubenhof they told me they had dispensed with keeping a bull some years before my time there. It was so difficult organising the mount. You were never sure if nature would do the trick. They had switched to artificial insemination. A vet, Gerhard laughed, with a big syringe, and he made an obscene gesture.

I peep into a couple of restaurant windows, but the interiors are too stiff, too wooden. Dark benches, antlers on the walls, a stuffed eagle. I didn't follow up my questions about Lawrence's ideas because I knew Julia didn't want me to. She wanted to hear herself talk about her research and where she would publish it and how Lawrence at least in this regard had been proved right. She wanted to feel confident and convinced. I wanted that too. But at some point I did say: I suppose what we have to decide, you know, is whether we're going to let Catherine ruin our lives.

I remember we were drinking more than we usually did. Julia particularly. That sour white wine.

No word from John? I asked.

John had his own world, she said. For a while she ate in silence and I knew there were thoughts she wasn't sharing. I splashed more wine into her glass and she began to say that we must find a path that kept us away from the autobahn. The sound of the traffic would drive her mad. It was so ironic, she said, that Lawrence's route had been buried under an avalanche of asphalt.

Away from the main street, there is nothing in Altdorf. Eventually I find the railway station, a Coop and a big concrete shelter with a couple of buses. It's all as grey and geometric as they come. Nowhere to eat, though. A fast train shrieks through without stopping. As the din fades you pick up the roar of the road drifting across the valley. On one wall of the bus shelter someone has spray-painted a

William Tell in the same pose as the statue in the square, but with a boombox on his shoulder. His son is wearing a baseball cap, munching an apple. Fortunately the Coop is open and I can pick up food for tomorrow's walk. At the till a dishevelled woman keeps the cashier talking while the queue gets longer and longer.

Will I have to go back to my room and eat bread and cheese? I'm beginning to wonder if I have the energy to go on with this journey. As if there were only bleakness and emptiness ahead. Perhaps it's just the weather. A few yards from my hotel I finally realise that the Wilhelm Tell Pizzeria has a garden. A peal of laughter from behind a high wall gives it away. What a stroke of luck. The other side of the building, next to the pizzeria and sharing the same garden, is the Thall Pub, which hits the spot exactly.

I take a table and settle down to watch young people drinking and talking in the failing light: some leaning forward; some listening with bright faces; some in the shadows. I remember Edwin Myer's wife, Barbara, that evening in Lucerne, his second wife rather, throwing those sidelong glances at me, while all the evening's conversation flew back and forth between her husband and Julia. We are spectators here, those glances said.

The waiter brings me my burger and beer. There's a pleasant atmosphere in the beer garden as darkness deepens in the valley and a low wall lighting comes on. A girl a couple of tables away is speaking louder than the others. They don't seem to be locals. I watch their animated faces. At another table two couples have four daughters between them, one looking around with restless eyes. What became of the Grubenhof girls? I wonder. I remember how their mother always had a benevolent smile for me. As if she pitied me. Just a little. She knew I wasn't cut out for farm life. I wasn't the son she wished she'd had. Drinking too much that last evening in the stodgy restaurant with the antlers and the dusty eagle and a second bottle of sour wine, I tried to cheer Julia up with more tales of my incompetence: how I'd fallen off a trailer load of hay bales, how I'd nearly lost a finger feeding grass into the shredding machine. As in fact Gerhard had some years before. Poor Danny, she said distractedly. And I realised it wasn't working. It was stupid.

I reached across the table and took her hand. I'm not poor Danny, I said. Not at all. Look at me. I have you, don't I? I'm lucky Danny, for Christ's sake, and we're so lucky to have found each other. Aren't we? We have a wonderful walk ahead of us. Right? A wonderful house to return to. A wonderful life.

She looked up, but her eyes were dazed, baffled. I was overcome by a sense of urgency.

You said you wanted a rock, right? Well, I'm here, Julia. I really am. I'm *real*. Touch me. I pulled her hand gently towards me. Come on. Lean on me. Hide in me.

Her fingers were limp. She looked across a table as though from a vast distance, further away even than the bedraggled eagle on the wall behind her. But I was absolutely determined.

You say you want to break out and live freely? We'll do it. We'll be completely open with each other. You'll tell me anything you want to tell me, have any argument you need to have. I don't care. Really. Shout at me. Whatever. Tear your hair. Throw me in the lion's den. Put me to the test. I'll never let you down. Never.

Dan, she whispered.

Then John and Catherine will see you're happy. They'll see you're free, and that you're really yourself. They're smart kids. They'll come round. And before they do I'll soak up anything they care to hit me with. Anything. Okay? I'll be kind and calm. I'll make things easy. For you. For us. Always. We'll come through and we'll be happy. Which is what this is all about, isn't it, why we've made all this effort.

Come through? she asked. She seemed to wake up a little. Her eyes were closer.

Right. We'll come through and it will be worth it. We'll be new together and happy. Our real selves.

That's incredible, she muttered.

It's already been incredible for four beautiful years.

No, I mean that you said, come through. She sighed. It was an expression that Lawrence used, the title of some poems, about him and Frieda: *Look, We Have Come Through.*

There you are then! I cried. I'll be a poet for you. Don't underestimate me. I gave her a wry grin. I have an old guitar somewhere. I'll write songs for you, I really will.

At last her hands came alive in mine. Our fingers twined. She was smiling through tears.

And there was me thinking you were tone deaf, she mocked. She wriggled her hand free. Now let's get out of this miserable place, before that bird spooks me altogether.

*

102

In bed I'm rereading Lawrence's meeting with the Eng-lishman. *My heart was wrung for my countryman, wrung till it bled.* Could it be he was hamming it? I ask myself. Was it meant to be funny? The sheer doggedness of this office clerk. Tramping over the mountains. Lawrence's wild exasperation. *Suddenly I hated him.* Why did Julia send me these pages? I wonder. After all these years. Or have her son send them. Eighteen sheets of paper, crumpled and fingered, with here and there an underlining. It happened very quickly, he replied, the son that is, John, when finally I tracked down an email address to thank him. Headaches, a tumour. Is it fanciful to suppose she wanted me to finish the walk that ended for us in Altdorf? We stumbled back to Zum Schwarzen Löwen and collapsed into a drunken sleep. Until, in the early hours, I was awoken by that unfor-gettable shriek. No! No, no, no!

And this time it wasn't a dream.

'So he had walked on and on, like one possessed'

JÜNGLING
LUDWIG ARNOLD

run the words on an iron cross beside the path from Alt-dorf to Erstfeld

GEBOREN 14. FEBRUAR 1952

Just five years before I was born . . .

VERUNGLÜCKTE
AN DIESER STELLE

I don't know the word *verunglückte*, but it can only mean one thing. *An dieser Stelle* – In this place. Meaning the river, I suppose, the Reuss, flowing fast and grey to my left.

AM 20 JUN 1958

Dead at six. About the age Tell's boy was when he faced his father across the square. I passed the statue again leaving Altdorf a couple of hours ago: the hero looking up towards the mountains, the *Jüngling* looking up at his father. I like the word *Jüngling*. Do we know his name? Once or twice I've tried to think about that moment as I walk. The crossbow and the apple. The unknown in the equation has to be their emotions. Tell is a renowned marksman. But this is his son. Can the boy keep still? Much depends on how much he trusts his father. Are the Tells a happy family? Wilhelm places the bolt on the bow and raises it to his shoulder. He has to do this now. Before the child flinches. You have one chance. Whoosh.

Ryan will get another chance, Catherine. Of course he will. But not with us. There has to be some consequence for what he did.

Keep going anyway. That is the lesson I learned, or began to learn, that morning in Altdorf years ago. You give up or keep going. Perhaps it's not so much a choice as a disposition. And it hardly matters where you go. Just keep moving. So I set the alarm for five thirty, this morning, ate a yoghurt, shouldered my pack, and set out to find the Hohe Weg, up on the western side of the valley.

From here on, it's all new. First the outskirts of the town. Along Pro Familiaweg. A ruined tower to my right. Then a sharp climb, the valley misty under white cloud. Every mile or so along the trail there is a panel with a black-and-white photo and information in four languages. The Higher Way was built in 1959 so that pedestrians en route from Lucerne to the Gotthard could avoid a flood area. A major investment, the text enthuses, because it involved blasting a ninety-metre tunnel through the cliff above the river.

The tunnel is fun, bending this way and that, very narrow. There's a switch at the entrance that turns on a string of lights. The rock is rough hewn and you can see the mica sparkling in the granite. But because of the arduous detour, the panel concludes, the trail declined in significance. In fact, in an hour and more's walking I've seen no one.

After a while you climb down to the river again and there's the iron cross where Ludwig Arnold was carried off in the tumultuous waters of the Reuss. And now the autobahn strides overhead on giant pillars. Great blue girders just a few feet above. *Verunglückte*. We were up there, on the tarmac, racing to Zürich, shortly after dawn. Julia must have left her phone on through the night. I didn't hear it vibrate. Only her scream. The taxi left us at the airport shortly after eight. There was a British Airways flight at eleven. Only seats available in Business Class. Peter will be waiting at Arrivals, she told me. Best if we go out separately.

Again the path offers a panel. Only now does it occur to me that the theme of all this information is communication. Same with yesterday's speaking tubes. The Gotthard autobahn was completed in 1986, making the upper Reuss valley accessible for day trips. As I read, the noise of the rushing river mingles with the rumble of heavy vehicles. Local roads were freed from through traffic.

However, noise and air pollution compromised the quality of life and the hospitality industry lost many customers.

It's admirable, I suppose, how pride in achievement is tempered by sober realism. So the hiker, whose walk is not as beautiful as he hoped, has the consolation of grasping the broader picture behind his disappointment. A national referendum in 1958. Strenuous local resistance. The Seelisberg Tunnel opening in 1980. Zürich just an hour away. Consoled by the thought that you now understand how all this happened, you put resentment behind you and move on.

But is there any consolation for that morning's *verunglückte*? Have I ever understood what happened? Heavy footsteps hurrying along the corridor. Julia sobbing, Cathy, Cathy. Three sharp knocks. *Entschuldigung.* Bad news from home. I opened the door an inch. We need a taxi as soon as possible. At first I thought it must have been Peter had called. The evening's wine had left me with a pounding headache. Only in the Seelisberg Tunnel did it come out it was the Buddhist centre. A train accident. The woman didn't have much English. She's dead, oh she's dead, Julia moaned. But didn't she take the bus, I said stupidly, when she went to Wales? Julia asked the driver to stop. She needed to vomit. While I queued at the ticket counter, she spoke to Peter till her phone battery ran out. I moved her SIM to my phone. Staring at the departures board, I wondered at the speed with which we had found ourselves back at the airport. Our days of walking, the vast landscape, the long steamer ride, all wiped out in ninety minutes. Only later, contemplating the plane's heavy undercarriage as we climbed the gangway, did it dawn on me that Catherine hadn't been *on* the train. It wasn't that kind of accident.

Why didn't you confide in me? At Erstfeld I cross the river. The surprisingly modern clock on the old church tower says 8.30. Why didn't you speak the horror at once? We'll be completely open with each other, I had said. Only the night before. A couple with a child in a pushchair give me directions to a café. Come In, We're Open, says the sign. In English. But you closed yourself up. You spoke to Peter for an hour and more, pacing back and forth between check-in desks. But not to me. I take a seat out on the patio where there's a pink crocheted doily on every stone table-top. The customers are middle-aged and paunchy, check shirts and short trousers, chatting over morning coffee. Not a word during the flight. Rocking back and forth on your seat. Knuckle in your mouth. My only ever flight in Business Class. But a lover can hardly complain in these circumstances. He sorts out the taxi, buys the tickets, gives her his phone, picks up two bottles of water and a pack of paracetamol. I'll never let you down, I had told her.

Café crème und Nussgipfel, bitte.

Everything about this café is charming. Menus in child-ish handwriting, with cute crayon drawings. A twig broom propped against the wall to sweep the patio. On each table a pot of herbs, placed in the centre of the pink doilies. And a piece of polished quartz, from the heart of the mountains. In Grubenhof we used twig brooms to sweep the farm-yard every Saturday afternoon. Woe betide you if there was so much as a speck of dirt, a shred of straw, between the cobbles when you finished. A place where animals pissed and shat, where grass was shredded, hay pitched into the barn loft, where suppliers unloaded sacks and boxes and little girls played with their pet rabbits. Why won't you speak to me? I remember repeating over and over on the plane. But silently, to myself. Why won't you tell me what you know? I didn't feel I could say it out loud. Why won't you sob on my shoulder? The farmer pulled his pipe from his mouth and shook his head. *Das ist nicht sauber. Noch einmal.* Gerhard would sing while he swept. *Mädchen* and *Strümpfen.* Sometimes, surreptitiously, he took a swig from a hip flask. I never told Julia what became of Gerhard.

From Erstfeld to Silenen to Amsteg. It's all very well saying we need to find a route away from the autobahn, but how? The mountains each side are steep and dark. How can you make progress if you leave the valley? Now I'm by the river again, climbing slowly as the water rushes towards me. Railway construction produced a huge amount of excavated material, says panel number 38, which was transported away over this temporary military bridge, built in 1936. Steel girders span the grey water. Eighty-six temporary years. This won't last, I told myself on the plane. It's a trial. Perhaps every life has an ordeal that defines a before and after. Put me to the test, I had told her. If only I had known what would be asked of me. At passport control we had to queue. Then she asked me to wait a few minutes before going out. If I went first Peter might recognise me.

Lawrence is eloquent on this stage of the journey. *So I set off up the valley between the close, snow-topped mountains, whose white gleamed above me as I crawled, small as an insect, along the dark, cold valley below.* There are no snowy peaks this morning. Only cloud. Feeling no smaller than I usually do, I cross the railway and climb the slope. The valley's eastern flank. A goat is sitting on the roof of a shed, occasionally jangling the bell on his neck. ACHTUNG KINDER says a sign at the entrance to a farmyard. There are graphic silhouettes of a boy kicking a ball, a girl with a skipping rope. Did the Grubenhof girls skip? I don't think so. Elsewhere, a huge old tractor tyre has been populated with gnomes wearing pointy hats. Names and birthdays above a farmhouse door. Elias. Timo. Marigolds and geraniums. All stations on the Gotthard railway, says panel 37, were built to a standard design made by the architect Gustav Mossdorf. This is Silenen. However, switch points and signals are now operated remotely. On a windowsill old boots serve as flowerpots. A stone drinking trough is smothered in moss. These details are providential. Keep moving, I tell myself. You're not a rock.

Einen Apfelsaft, bitte. On the terrace of a café flying the Canton Uri flag a bald man in cycling gear has his face low over a plate of chips. He laughs and says something with a full mouth. Fleeing to the furthest table, I sip my *Saft* and nibble my sandwiches. The red ring in the bull's nose is irksome. Julia ate nothing on the flight, and I kept her hungry company. At Arrivals I hurried after her as soon as she was out of sight. A chasm was opening up. She was gone. Only late that evening, one message: I think I'm dying, Dan.

While eating I try to find a place to sleep this evening. I'm booking same day now, since it's hard to be sure how far I'll get. My knee is uncomfortable on downward slopes. But there's nothing available in the valley. It's Saturday. Everything's taken. Why didn't I think of this? Eventually, I settle on a room with shared toilet, near Gurtnellen, two thousand feet above the valley floor, on the western side. Rather than strike up there from directly below, six or seven miles on, I decide to leave the Gotthard trail now, at Amsteg, and work my way south along the mountainside. This is clearly unwise because it is coming on to rain. But nothing seems more urgent than to do something unwise. Checking the exact location on Booking.com, I see there is a message for me. Herr Burrow, you are leaving an umbrella in my apartment. If you tell me an address I will send. Frau Schönauer (Heike), Jestetten. The odd thing is I didn't pack an umbrella. Only a waterproof.

Once again I cross the Reuss, then go under the autobahn just before it disappears into the mountain. Milano 190 km. I can read the sign from below. White letters on green. The area is fenced off. On the other side, stone steps take me up the embankment beside the tunnel mouth, cars hurtling in, cars hurtling out. Then you climb upwards into the woods. Altogether a smaller path now. No tourist-board panels here. It's steep and damp and cluttered with twigs and pinecones. *So he walked on and on, like one possessed*, says Lawrence of his Englishman. Something like that. *Though it were torture, his body must pay what his will demanded.* On the tube to Chiswick Park I realised: Julia will have to see the body.

Did I really need to come here to remember this stuff? Surely it would have been enough to take public transport to Gunnersbury and stare at the house on Oxford Road South. All my savings invested in our future. With bedrooms for the children. As Julia insisted. Should they so desire. I remembered years ago being delayed on a train that hit someone on the line. When finally we started moving, the police had erected a kind of tent and two firemen were hosing down the shale by the track. It's important not to see these things. Now Julia was going through this horror without me beside her. If there's anything I can do, any way I can help? I texted. She was going through it with Peter. She didn't reply. A husband whose ordinariness was a blight. I felt the distance opening up between us. Surprisingly fast. The way you reach a break in the trees, turn back and see the valley is already far below, the Reuss snaking round the base of hills and the autobahn snaking with it, in and out of tunnels, road and river crossing and re-crossing each other, as if plaited together. But already it hardly makes much sense looking back. Up ahead someone has built a treehouse on a high meadow. Or rather, hung a platform between tree and cliff and built a wooden hut up there, in the air. A child's dream. And far above, on a high spur projecting from the same cliff, there's a cross. Misty in the cloud. A crucifix. I would never have dreamed of letting Rachel call me Dan. We were father and daughter. It was the only way our relationship made sense. For all its awkwardness. Suddenly it seemed astonishing that I knew so little about Mr Ingram and his family. The stockbroker of Italian ancestry. Of course, Julia had spoken about driving John to his swimming competitions; she had told me how upset she was when Catherine gave up her dance class, when she cut off her long hair. The children were close to their father, she said. She couldn't contemplate breaking up the family before they were independent. Why had Catherine done this?

For years, I realised, returning to Oxford Road South that evening, you have been living beside a powder keg. I was appalled by my carelessness. You bought this house on a cliff edge. Or had it been the merest accident? The girl had slipped on the station platform. That was it. I still couldn't believe she was dead. Smoking dope, perhaps. Or drinking. I never think of Margaret's death as anything but an accident. It's crazy to suppose she would have crashed on purpose. As soon as I was through the door I fired up my laptop and typed Catherine Ingram into Google. Up came a Facebook page. Inactive for a year and more. Train, I typed, Accident, Wales. Sure enough a Glamorganshire website had a Tragedy at Pontypridd Station. Shortly before midnight. A goods train. An as yet unnamed woman. That would be 1 a.m. in Altdorf. Circumstances under investigation. I wasn't sure where the Buddhist community was exactly. I couldn't remember its name. Barbara Myers hadn't been impressed. Catherine was so determined to provoke, I thought. My mum smokes dope, she said. In front of the class. Determined to right wrongs. To impose her will on the world, perhaps. I blew him a kiss, she said. To the maths teacher who was grooming a friend. She claimed. Then suddenly withdrew to a Buddhist community. She always gives up the things she's good at, Julia said. But who could have predicted this? With her nail-bitten fingers and hollow cheeks. I felt sick.

I'm walking on grass now. It's wet and steep. High pastureland. A baita far above looks like it might slither down at any moment. There are spots of rain in the air. *The villages on the slopes seemed they must slide down and tumble to the water course*, Lawrence thought. To the Reuss. *And be rolled away, away to the sea*. Like Ludwig Arnold. The *Jüngling*. Please Julia, I replied when her message came that evening, please don't do anything rash. I love you. I'm here for you.

My foot slips and I grab a branch. Deciduous has given way to pine. The raindrops are fatter and heavier. Or perhaps I'm in the cloud now. How awful must it be to see a child's mangled body? For Peter too, poor man. They were going through this hell together. They were man and wife. Late at night, wandering through the empty rooms in Oxford Road South, I suddenly thought I would go mad. I suddenly understood what jealousy is. Why had I never called her Jewel? But how stupidly petty of me. How shameful. They had lost a child. If Tell had missed, he had a spare bolt ready to dispatch the tyrant, Hermann Gessler. So he later said. If Margaret and I had lost Rachel? It was unthinkable. I needed someone to talk to. The thoughts just kept on churning. Urgently. Catherine was dead. But who? I had surrendered my friends when we went to Yorkshire, to the boarding school. In London there was only Julia. For years life had been school and Julia. Planning for this moment, saving for this house. I could hardly phone Rachel and say, Remember when you thought I was seeing a woman? Years ago. Well, now her daughter has killed herself. Because of us.

I'm standing by a stream. A folly of white water tumbles between great black and brown boulders, smooth and shiny with erosion, like a panic of fat pigs stampeding down the mountainside. The path crosses the feature on a rope bridge. You can imagine if one of these rocks were dislodged. They must already have rolled a long way to get where they are. You have the impression of some natural calamity that has been interrupted, frozen. The stampeding swine magically stilled. Only the water crashing over their smooth backs. But at any moment the avalanche will resume.

Because of us. Surely she couldn't think that.

Just the other side of the stream, there is something that looks like a bird box, an old splintery thing on a wooden post, blue paint flaking away. A steel cable keeps it anchored to the rock. Inside is a tiny stone Madonna. A tutelary presence. Delicately carved. Sitting on a throne, wearing a crown. But her weathered face is gone, blank. Likewise her child's. Her throne is cracked. Please, I prayed that night, I who never pray, please don't let her think it's because of us.

But now I have a navigation problem. In the woods the path was obvious enough. There was only one place to cross the stream. Now I'm high up on mossy grass, in the mist, with giant granite outcroppings. Patches of fern. The rock protrudes every which way in odd shapes and spikes, with no logic, as if below the soil there were another mad tumbling of broken stuff. The path isn't so clear here. No one passes this way. I can't find the painted red-and-white flashes, on stone or tree, that should be showing the way. There is only the small blue arrowhead on my phone, my position on the map. It's raining hard now. When the screen gets wet the phone freezes. The battery is low. Water is streaming off my waterproof. I look up to study the landscape. The shape of the contours. There's a fence post, perhaps – is there? – way above, where the trees start again. I'm shivering. And suddenly very, very happy I came this way. What more could a geography teacher ask?

I asked Rachel to lunch. She had news, a new man she had met. Isn't this house too big for you? she asked. She seemed a different person. Weren't you supposed to be on a walking holiday? Not a word about her mother, whom she much resembles. And differs from. There was something fresh and carefree in her manner. Problem with my knee, I said. I was at a loss to explain myself. At a loss to find a way forward. The idea of asking her why she had once said her mother's death was not an accident seemed grotesque.

Are you okay? she enquired. There was a moment's curiosity. Her round face cocked to one side, eyes clouding. But she had so much to tell. Useful work experience at Nine Elms. She had joined a choir. I had never seen her so cheerful. Yet couldn't respond. As soon as she was gone I took an umbrella and walked towards the river. To Grove Park Road. It was only a few minutes. That's why I had bought in Chiswick. So her children could have both parents close by. I knew the street, but not the number. I had been careful never to come this way. Now I went when it was most inappropriate. When there was nothing to be achieved by going. By going to Grove Park Road, I realised, I am simply announcing my loss of nerve, my loss of trust. I am saying, Why aren't you writing to me, Julia? Why haven't you phoned? When it's obvious why she is not writing. She is overwhelmed by grief. Perhaps guilt. She is going through a major life experience, without me. I was surprised by the quality of the housing in Grove Park Road. The sheer size of the properties. All set well back from the street. Freestanding. Gravel drives with three or four cars. It was her car I was hoping to recognise. Her blue Audi. With the pearlescent finish. A gift from Peter when she got her lectureship. That we had kissed in so often. There was no sign of it. Very likely it was parked in Pontypridd.

How ridiculous, I mutter. Something happens and you discover you are ridiculous. You look at the landscape, make your plans, then the avalanche begins to slide. *It seems as though some dramatic upheaval must take place*, Lawrence reflected, climbing the Reuss valley, *the mountains must fall down into their own shadows*. I've seen no sign of the path now for twenty minutes and more. No red-and-white flashes. But I'm not dismayed. I'm enjoying being wet. I'm glad my boots are soaked, tramping over the mossy grass between the granite outcrops. Just below the fence now. A string of wooden posts with a single wire. The merest demarcation, between open slope and forest. Where there is a fence there is civilisation, communication. Some of the trees have been felled. There will be a forest track, to take the timber down to the valley. *The valley beds were like deep graves*, Lawrence thought. *The sides of the mountains like the collapsing walls of a grave.*

Funeral tomorrow, Julia texted. Forgive the long silence.

You are constantly in my thoughts, my love. Can't wait to see you.

Poor Danny, she replied.

I told the Gasthaus Bergheim I would arrive around four. I'm going to be late. But I am back on the path. Or a path. I spotted a line of telegraph poles, a sagging cable. Worked my way up there, through scree and fern. On hands and knees at one point. My jeans are drenched. Sure enough there's a track. A farm building. Wooden walls and a corrugated iron roof. A dog barking. I had hoped I might recognise Bobbie in Grove Park Road. The poles carry the cable southward, round the mountain, following the contour. But no such luck. It's easy walking now. With a sheer drop to the left. No doubt a magnificent view, if only the cloud would lift. Everything is wraithlike. You can't see how far you would fall. Then at last a substantial building: the Maria Hilf Kapelle. 1712. White in the greyness. Built against a bank of granite. Hay bales wrapped in white plastic stacked alongside. Such things were unimaginable when I laboured at Grubenhof. Likewise phones with maps that tell you your battery is now critical. Inside, the chapel has been freshly renovated. There are fresh flowers on the altar, below a baroque Mary framed in gold. To one side is a wooden rack with rows of red candles in shallow glass jars. Two boxes of matches and a money box. Make a donation and light a candle. I'm not tempted. But couldn't resist the urge to go to Grove Park Road that evening. Again. The funeral would be in London, surely. Couldn't resist poking my nose into the driveways. To spy the Mercedes and the Maseratis. Or her beloved collie. Pointed gables behind tall trees. Cedars and limes and horse chestnuts. Then at last the familiar Audi. It was a sober three-storey Georgian house. BMW convertible beside. A balmy summer evening. Brown brickwork, black drainpipes. The hedge had been recently trimmed. The door recently repainted, shiny. Curtains drawn over symmetrical sash windows. Ordinarily beautiful, I thought. Ordinarily expensive. An immense desire to walk in and announce myself. Horror at the thought.

A puddle is forming at my feet, in the stillness of the Maria Hilf Kapelle. Saints and Madonna presiding. Outside the rain hasn't let up. I need to be on the move. I need to get to Gasthaus Bergheim before my phone dies. Water is gurgling down the farm track. Carrying mud and pine needles down to the Reuss. My path is all downhill now. Past cows huddled in a corner where two walls meet. A clanging of bells when they struggle to their feet. Wary of this man looming from the mist. Dan, she wrote, I'm going to go to Bodhikusuma for one of their retreats. I want to be where Catherine was.

Now I'm contemplating a huge muddy puddle. All this happened long ago, of course. There seems to be no way round it. Yet keeps on happening. It's a pond almost, but I splash straight in. What choice do I have? Could I come too? I asked. To the retreat? At least be near you, in silence? Perhaps so long as we're alive all that has happened to us can keep on happening. Maybe freezes for a few years, then starts to slide again. Be patient, Dan. I'm turning the phone off now, for a week or two. I won't miss our messaging, I had told her on the steamer from Konstanz to Schaffhausen. Only days before. I remember that moment so clearly. I will not miss sending messages, I had said. How sure of myself I had been! When had Julia ever turned her phone off? On the very last step my right foot sinks deep and water floods over the boot. Laughing, I put the other beside it and stamp my feet.

Now I do have a choice. There's the farm track, winding into the valley in loops and hairpins, and a path that plunges straight down across steep wet meadow. Knee and ankle are warning me to take the track. Be patient, Dan. There will be plenty of time for doing something rash. Holed away in Oxford Road South, where there was still so much work to do, bedrooms to decorate, damp to fix, I looked up Bodhikusuma. On Google. These were the days when we should have been in Italy, when we should have been becoming a couple, in Florence and Rome. Flower of enlightenment, the word means. The community's site has photographs of people cross-legged in rows. Blank faces, faint smiles. A garden with rhododendrons and a golden Buddha. There are ten levels of awareness. *Bhaya*, fear of the arising of mind and matter. *Muncitukamyata*, desire for cessation of matter and mind. How will I pay the mortgage, I wondered, if I end up living here alone?

Exact money in the jar, please. At a turn in the track there's a small wooden hut. Utterly isolated, utterly solitary. GORNERALP GURTNELLEN, says a piece of paper taped behind the window. SELF SERVICE. The door is open. An antique handcart serves as a counter. A fridge with soft drinks and local cheeses. You take and pay. *Herzlichen Dank* handwritten on a round stone beside a jar that has a couple of coins in the bottom. Stepping inside, it's strange how similar to the church it is: motionless objects waiting for the unlikely visitor, anxious to have you spend some money, for a cheese or a candle.

I go back outside and find the landscape has changed. In a matter of seconds. The cloud has dropped down into the valley. Everything below me is a sea of white. All around and above are the slanting peaks, vast tracts of stone and scree, pine and pasture, glistening in the sunlight, streaked with snow. My phone sends its death rattle. Turning off in thirty seconds. But rising through the cloud, some distance to my right is the red dome of a church. And sure enough a clock face. Gurtnellen.

Mein Gott!

Gasthaus Bergheim is all black shingles outside, varnished pine within, and hanging baskets dripping small blue flowers and red tablecloths and antlers and rows of coloured bottles.

Ich bin Herr Burrow.

She bursts out laughing. A solid forty-year-old with steamy glasses, wiping her hands on her apron, shaking with laughter. *Sie sind pudelnass!* she cries. Drenched to the bone.

And I begin to laugh too. No doubt I do look pretty funny. Then the laughter turns to sobs. I have to turn away. My hostess hurries to bring me a bowl of barley soup.

'The hideous rawness of the world of men'

Directly across the valley from my window in Gasthaus Bergheim, perhaps a half-mile as the crow flies, the sheer cliff face is scarred by what I assume is an old avalanche, a great grey gash in the mountain. Only gazing out there for some minutes, do I realise it is actually a quarry. There are four or five yellow excavators on a great heap of rubble at the base. A zigzag pattern in the rock above. You have avalanches on the brain, I tell myself, stretching out on a narrow bed: landslides, tumbling water, drownings, breakdowns. It seems bizarre to me that I should break down and sob like a child in the Reception of a remote mountain hostel, when I shed not a single tear, that I recall, lying on my bed in Oxford Road South years ago. Rather I turned my attention to the extensive house decorations that would have to be done before Julia moved in. Perhaps with John, if he so desired. Catherine is dead, I told myself. Catherine will never come. Julia will never get over it. How do you get over the death of a daughter? The suicide of a daughter? If suicide it was. All the same, I must trust her, I decided. I must believe we will come through. Like her hero Lawrence. Come through despite everything. Receiving an email from the clerk of the school governors summoning me to an extraordinary meeting of the board the following Monday, I remember feeling pleased that some work distraction would see me through these empty days, the first in four and more years when I had not either seen Julia or exchanged a score of messages with her. I caught myself compulsively checking my phone, astonished to find its little screen empty. In Gasthaus Bergheim I plug in the phone charger, carry my wet clothes to the drying room, and head downstairs for dinner.

The place is packed. Who would have thought? It's not just a Gasthaus but a restaurant. Full of locals. The men sit with their feet well part, their elbows on the tables. There is steam in the air, a buzz of Saturday-night wellbeing. Frau Bittli is a celebrated cook. So it says on the Gasthaus website. At least in this neck of the woods. Now she is at a loss to know where to seat me. There is a family of Germans and a large group of loud men, burly and tattooed, who I assume must be bikers. I can see at once she has taken a liking to me. It's the same kind of motherly sympathy I somehow inspired in my hostess in Jestetten. I'm the kind of man who seems in need of moral support. Eventually she places me at a table where a young couple are already sitting, by the wall, talking urgently in Yorkshire accents. I refuse to be a slave, the boy is saying. *Ich hätte gern die Knödel*, I tell Frau Bittli.

If you feel you need psychological support, Mrs Waring murmured as I stood up to leave the extraordinary meeting of the board of governors, I would be more than happy to arrange that for you. The only woman present had felt a certain sympathy, despite the shadow that now hung over me. There are provisions in these cases, she explained. Thank you, but that won't be necessary, I told her. *Dankeschön*, I tell Frau Bittli when she brings the dumplings and a bottle of beer. Turning it round I find the name Feldschlösschen. It's the same beer I used to drink on the sly with Gerhard at Grubenhof. The label hasn't changed in all these years. How scattered one's life becomes, across time and space, how hard to gather it up into anything definite. The beer tastes wonderful, in the steamy air of Gasthaus Bergheim. As it did beside a steamy pile of cow shit in Grubenhof. I smack my lips and feel positive.

At no point do the young couple acknowledge my presence. They have ordered a second half-litre of wine. I might be a ghost. The boy is a massive fellow. Hearty, earnest, petulant. He feels he's overworked, he says. He wants out. He would prefer a job in the open air. His pupils suck him dry, the endless assessments are bugging him, the endless homework to mark. He chose the wrong profession. Across the table, his young woman listens, interrupts, listens, interrupts. They are not wearing rings. She is altogether more sure of herself. What kind of outdoor job? she asks. Gardener? Mountain guide? As if she were offering professional advice. It's not clear to me whether the boy is accepting this superiority or resisting it. They look more or less the same age, mid-twenties, yet she is a woman while he is a boy. He is accepting *and* resisting it, I decide. He's struggling against an obvious reality. She is emphatic, authoritative. I wonder what she does exactly. Meantime, they both have extraordinary appetites, tucking away first the dumplings, then schnitzel and chips. Their faces are flushed with exercise and youth and drink. There's a shine on them. I'm loving it. I'm lapping up their accents. What a surprise to hear Yorkshire in the Gasthaus Bergheim. Neither of them have tattoos, I notice. Both send messages while they talk, while they eat, while they drink their wine. She shows him a photo, on her phone. He reads out a friend's comment. There's never a second's space. Listen to what Garry says, he laughs. Garry back home presumably. Could it be Middlesbrough? Darlington? Malton even? Where Margaret drove her car into the back of a stationary lorry. High speed and heavy spray from oncoming vehicles the likely causes, said the police report. No rain tomorrow, the young woman tells her boy. She has the weather up on her phone. I love the rain, he says. I'd love to work in the rain.

I stand up to pay. People are paying at the till. *It is difficult to get a sense of the native population*, Lawrence thought, *dwelling in the tang of snow and the noise of icy water*. Frau Bittli smiles warmly and offers me a schnapps on the house. *But distracted by hotels, foreigners, parasitism*. Don't drink when you're sad, a voice warns me. I'm not sad, a louder voice retorts. How can one possibly be sad in a busy, steamy restaurant with people shouting in half a dozen languages after a long day in the mountain air, after surviving the rain and the rocks and the low clouds? The schnapps is fierce. I have to shut my eyes, I'm so pleased to be here, in the thick of it.

You wanted to plunge into life, I told myself, leaving the extraordinary meeting of the board of governors, when you started your affair with Julia. You wanted at last to be in the thick of it, after the long hibernation in Yorkshire, the deadness of the last years with Margaret. And now you are in the shit up to your eyeballs.

In the early hours I have to get up for a pee. The schnapps has left my mouth dry. The bathroom is the other end of the corridor. The floorboards squeak. From behind one door come the unmistakable moans of lovemaking. Is it the couple from Yorkshire? They were so appealing. Why do I feel a vague apprehension for them? As if they were walking on the edge of a precipice. Or am I seeing an avalanche where actually there is a quarry? We certainly won't be jumping to any conclusions, Dan, the chair of the board assured me. You know that in general we couldn't be more satisfied with your performance. But you understand it may take time to complete our inquiries.

My room is all pine panelled, with clunky pine furniture, twin beds, orange curtains. There is a strong resiny smell. Even the ceiling is clad with pine. As if one were to sleep inside a tree. Despite the hour, I open the window and lean out into the night. You can't see the bottom of the valley, the autobahn and the railway and the factories, only woods dropping away steeply and the massive grey wall of the mountain opposite. There's no moon, but the sky is pulsing with points of white light. Constellations. Galaxies. There are so many. They feel so close. As the people in the dining room felt so close. As Julia seemed so close sometimes, even when she was far away, in the Bodhikusuma. Light years away. Was she checking her phone, I wondered, on the sly?

Returning from the meeting of the school board, I tried to prepare a message for her. I opened a bottle of wine and sat down at my desk. Someone has written a letter, I began. I would write on paper first and only transfer it to the phone when I was sure I had it right. Accusing me of inappropriate behaviour. I wasn't used to drinking on my own. But I felt I needed this support. The school has suspended me while they look into it. I tried to imagine her reading these words, after a long day sitting in silence, or listening to sermons about the arising of mind and matter. Surely she would want to stay in contact with John. And I was wondering, could it possibly be that . . . ?

You can't send this message, I realised. I poured another glass of wine. There was so much work still to be done in Oxford Road South. Most of my old furniture was unsuitable. My books were still in boxes. You can't tell me who is making this accusation? I asked the governors. They couldn't. You can't tell me what it is exactly I'm accused of? They shook their heads. Five men and one woman round a table meant for a dozen and more. But it was holiday time. Is it of a sexual nature? This was not something they felt authorised to disclose. Nor when. Nor where. Our first duty is to protect the young person involved, Dan. Should they eventually feel compelled to report the matter to the police, then the police would give me such details as I needed to defend myself.

I was wondering, Julia, if it could possibly be that Catherine . . .

If you send this message, I drained my glass and poured another, it will be the end of your relationship with Julia.

A woman grieving for a child who has died in the most dramatic and distressing circumstances. I emptied the bottle into my glass. A woman examining her own behaviour over recent years, perhaps, in the light of what has happened. If you put your own predicament before her grief, I thought, all trust between you will be finished.

Looking out over the Reuss valley, from my window on the second floor of the Gasthaus Bergheim, gazing up through the wonderfully fresh air at a firmament alive with points of white light, it seems remarkable to me that despite the quantities of alcohol I was getting through in those days, despite the yearning I felt, and the anger, the intense anger, I managed not to send that message. I would be loyal, I decided. I would accept her need for this period of withdrawal and mourning. It was more than understandable. Catherine was dead. And any day, any moment, the clerk of the board of governors would phone to tell me it had been a hoax. The revenge of some pupil suspended or disciplined. Ryan Hughes, perhaps. I had no record of bullying or suspect behaviour of any kind. Miss Walsh, I had said, on the one occasion when there had been a hint of impropriety on school premises, I don't think this is the time or place. How long had I been alone in my office with Catherine that day? Five minutes? Ten? It's true that even that was unusual and unwise. Would I have undertaken that interview alone if she had not been the daughter of my lover? Had I reacted guiltily, when the board informed me of a letter? What did they infer when I asked when the letter was dated, where it was posted from?

One unhappy evening I called Andy Robb, the maths

teacher. I pulled up his name on the screen, heard the phone begin to ring. And pressed the red button. I must not under any circumstances appear to be making inquiries. As if I knew of someone who might have reason to accuse me. Very soon Julia would be back. Somehow or other the matter would be raised. Just by answering her questions: Why are you not at work? Why are you drinking so much? But if the board of governors now knew that the person who wrote that letter – anonymous or signed? Handwritten or printed? – had been killed under a train soon after, what conclusions would they draw? She had died because of the behaviour she denounced. At which point they would feel compelled, surely, to report the matter to the police. And what would Julia infer? Catherine had died in a panic after denouncing me?

Mr Burrow? Sir?

It was Andy Robb's voice.

Mr Burrow, did you call?

I must have hesitated a moment. Sorry, Andy, I think the thing called by accident.

No worries, sir. It happens.

Again there was a short silence.

All well? he asked. Good holiday?

Would he know that I had been suspended? Term was weeks away. Had he written me an email and found my address deactivated?

Fine, I told him. Walking in the Swiss Alps. Yourself?

Sounds splendid, he said. We had a pretty tame time in Dorset. My two are quite young, you know.

I wondered if he could sense I had been drinking.

But we're home again now, he wound up, refreshed and raring to go. He wanted to close the call.

Right, I said. Back to kids blowing kisses at us.

It took him a second to catch on. It had been two years ago after all. Oh right, he agreed, what a weird one she was.

How stupid of me was it to make that allusion? Suddenly I'm aware I won't be able to sleep. This torrent is running too fast. I'm tempted to slip downstairs and take a stroll in the dark, under the stars. But doubtless there will be a dog to guard the Gasthaus Bergheim. I will wake people up. I stretch on the bed under the window and study the graining in the pine ceiling. The night is uncannily silent. Just occasionally a low hum, on and off. A pump perhaps. It was the silence that most disoriented me in the weeks after our return from Switzerland. I was used to working twelve-hour days, now there was nothing. I was used to handling fifty or a hundred emails. Now there were none. Julia did not get in touch. Retreats at the Bodhikusuma Meditation Centre vary from three days, for children, seven days for beginners, and one month for experienced yogis. So the website said. I wasn't familiar with the word yogi. A week had passed. A month seemed an impossibly long time. There was no point, I realised, in starting to redecorate the house, since this was surely something Julia would want to be involved in. Dan, I understand your anxiety, the chair of the governors replied to my email. I can only assure you that the instant our inquiries are complete you will be informed.

Silence is a space one falls into, it occurs to me, lying on top of the bedclothes, letting the cold air from the open window flow over me. Except there's no impact. Again I remember Julia's dream of the dog falling from the roof of the department store. How will this silence end? you wonder. As if someone had died in my place, she said.

I sit up on the narrow bed in the Gasthaus Bergheim. There's a glimmer of light in the room. Did she really say that? Why didn't I remember it before? Why can't I sleep? I don't want to read Lawrence, I decide, on the next leg of our journey. Not for the moment. As if someone had died in my place. I can even hear the voice she said it in. A low murmur. In the commuter train from Zürich to Kilchberg. Musing over her dream. One of those dreams that gets to you, she said. Teases you. Was she teasing me, sending me these pages, in extremis? Inviting me to look over the edge?

I change my mind, fish Lawrence out of my pack and turn on the bedside lamp. *It is the hideous rawness of the world of men, the horrible, desolating harshness of the advance of the industrial world upon the world of nature, that is so painful.* I don't want to read this stuff. Why not write to me directly, if she had something to say? Why send a few pages of an old book?

I turn the light off again. Silence is a space one fills as one falls. Waiting to hit bottom. It stretches out endlessly. During those summer days in Oxford Road South I filled the days with endless imaginings. Suicide notes in which Catherine invented lurid stories. Suicide notes in which she begged forgiveness. I imagined Julia in Peter's arms. How could I be sure she was in the Bodhikusuma Meditation Centre? She had confessed all and he had forgiven her. She had finally appreciated the joys of ordinariness. I imagined the bell ringing in the early hours and a sharp rap on the door, Police. There were days I couldn't believe the police hadn't come. Days I couldn't believe the silence could go on for so long. Or that I could find so much unhappiness to fill it. If I go to a lawyer, I thought, or to my union representative, I will have to explain about the affair. Starting a process that will lead to everything coming out. Which might be completely unnecessary if the letter is not from Catherine. I mustn't do that without discussing it first with Julia. I needed to find out who the letter was from. I couldn't see any way of doing this. I couldn't see any way forward at all. That didn't go through the neck of a wine bottle.

Just keep going, I tell myself, Go through all this now, tonight, in the Gasthaus Bergheim, and tomorrow you will walk with a lighter load. But I'm suddenly aware that my room has no pictures on the wall. Which is unusual, isn't it? For a hotel room. There's not a single decoration. Aside from a white doily on the bedside table. Otherwise everything is pine. A pine obsession. One strip slotted beside the next. For the man who pines. Oh please. All knotted and grained. From its growth on the mountainside. I let my eye move over the walls, the ceiling. Dark oval knots in the blond wood. Dead broken branches enfolded in new growth. Stacked for years beside the track. Before being sliced into planks. Ripples of graining round the knots. I remember our annual field trip to Scawton sawmill. A man explaining the difference between live knots and dead. Pushing out a dead knot to show the children a knothole.

Look, nowt there now, children! The dead thing pushed out of the live. But in a way all the more present for not being there, for leaving an emptiness. At a certain point Andy Robb called again. Our senior maths teacher. At a certain point I did write to Julia. I can't remember the exact sequence of events. There was the flight back to London. There was the governors' meeting. Walks to Grove Park Road. Too many. Bottles of wine. No particular preference. No sign of the Audi. No sign of Bobbie. Oceans of forgotten TV. The house on Oxford Road South was papered upstairs and down in a pale green pattern that I was eager to replace. I was eating badly. Dead-frog green, Julia had called it when she inspected the place. There was damp in the second bathroom. She would want to be involved in choosing the new colours. I couldn't be bothered to cook for myself. But knotholes can be covered by what we call veneer patches, the man at the sawmill explained. How all this useless stuff comes back! How's it going, Julia? I wrote. Are you checking your phone from time to time? I'm desperate to see you. I was calling about that girl who's died, sir, Andy Robb began. I remember feeling afraid as I tapped out those words to Julia. As if she were some kind of ogre and I were taking a terrible risk disturbing her. Oh yes? I asked. Instantly I was anxious I would say the wrong thing. Someone told me, he said, that Catherine Ingram – you remember? – has died. Silence. What should I say? Her brother won the Maths Prize this year. How had I got myself into a position where the simplest of reactions was impossible? Andy kept talking. If you are sending our condolences, sir, I was wondering if you might add mine, and mention my name. She was such a bright kid, even if she could be a pain. I was tongue tied. I'll do that, Andy, thanks. What a terrible thing, I said. Closing the call, I felt I must take the initiative. He hadn't mentioned suicide. Would there have been a coroner's verdict? Had the parents informed the school? I couldn't just go on waiting. Waiting to hit bottom. I must make a move. My present situation is intolerable, I wrote to the board of governors. If my suspension is not lifted before school resumes, I shall have no alternative but to resign. Catherine is top of the class in everything but maths, Julia had said. They were a competitive family. Apparently it galled the girl she wasn't top in maths as well. Like her little brother. A credit to your school. Then she dropped out of everything. I must go to Wales, I decided. I must go to the Bodhikusuma Meditation Centre and demand to know what Julia knows. What Catherine has written about me.

The curiosity of the pine wall cladding is how you look for a pattern but can't find one. The knots are similar, and the graining, the voluptuous curves round the knotholes, but there's no consistent arrangement. So you look harder. You want to find a pattern. There is none. No constellations. No bears great or small, or dogs or hunters. No reply from Julia. Weeks had passed. I felt dead, broken. Think through all this tonight, I tell myself. Come on, speed it up. Once and for all. You'll walk more easily tomorrow. Towards the Gotthard. Towards Italy. Get yourself seriously cold now, lying naked on top of the bed, under the open window, then when you cover yourself with the quilt you'll fall asleep. Strategies. I took the train and bus to Bodhikusuma. I don't have a car. I never learned to drive.

It was always Margaret who drove. Dear Mr Burrow, we understand your decision, replied the clerk of the board of governors. However, we believe the Local Authority Designated Officer will be interviewing you shortly.

Observe the Noble Silence, said a notice on the gate. There was a leafy path and an old gatekeeper's lodge. It was a charming place. It's urgent, I insisted. The man was European, German perhaps, but wearing a brown robe, his head shaven. I will go and speak to her, he said. Outsiders, he told me, were not allowed into the meditation centre during retreats. He was polite but firm. Why do I always obey the rules? I wondered. Why don't I burst in anyway? He was away twenty minutes and more. Julia does not wish to speak to you at the present moment, he said. She will write as soon as the retreat is over. On the trip back I was furious with myself for not having asked when the retreat ended.

Denial. I speak the word out loud. My skin is goose-pimpling under the window. Is there something obvious I have always denied? Obvious to everyone but me. Some essential fact about myself or my behaviour. About Julia too. And about Margaret. About teaching and about schools. About not having a driving licence. I want to be walking again. That is the truth. I want to sleep sound, wake up and walk on the mountains. Walk and walk and walk. I want the problems to be heat and cold, tiredness and hunger. I want my money to last for ever so I can walk for ever. Eating warm meals in steamy guesthouses, where other men and women argue and make love. This is the letter, said the Local Authority Designated Officer. She handed me a white envelope and a sheet of notepaper attached with a clip. School of Communication & Creativity, said the embossed heading. Her mother's paper. Dear governors. I could not believe this was happening, hadn't foreseen this possibility. My hands trembled. Out of control. Across the table three women were watching, and one young man. As I read the letter. They had pens and notepaper. Dear governors, I am writing to make a formal complaint about my old headmaster, Mr Burrow. The handwriting was absolutely even, perfectly horizontal. The letters very small, but also very clear and very neat. Perfect homework. I left the school two years ago, but the fact is Mr Burrow is destroying my life and my family. He took advantage of his position in the school to have an affair with my mother. This affair has been going on for many years. My mother is unable to escape from it. My father has been completely destroyed. My life will never be the same. I am asking you to intervene, please. Yours sincerely, Catherine Julia Ingram.

I continued to stare at the paper, my hands continued to shake. I had made no plans for this.

First, Mr Burrow – I'm shaking with cold under the open window on my narrow bed in the Gasthaus Bergheim – could you please tell us: is it a fact that you have a relationship with Catherine's mother?

I looked at the four people opposite. The Allegations Committee. Legend has it that LADOs have become a kind of witch hunt: prosecutor, judge and jury. The teacher is always presumed guilty, the child is always right. But I saw only sympathetic faces. I cast about for a professional response. Who I have relationships with, I began, outside school, is, I think, my own business. I stopped. With no warning I changed tack. Suddenly I had to put it out there. However, yes. Since you ask. Yes, I do. It's true.

It was not the answer they expected. There were a couple of ahs, a shuffling of papers, glances exchanged.

You are surprised?

The Designated Officer sighed deeply. Mr Burrow, you are aware that Catherine Ingram is no longer with us.

Of course.

Studying the pine ceiling in the Gasthaus Bergheim, the knots and the grains, I recall the enormous sense of relief I felt in sharing these truths.

You can imagine, then, that, in the circumstances, we felt obliged to contact her mother.

You have spoken to Julia, to Mrs Ingram?

She told us that Catherine was challenged in various ways and suffering from delusions.

There was a long silence around the table. How can I forget it? A silence that seems one with the silence in Gurtnellen. In the Gasthaus Bergheim. Shortly before dawn. Perhaps all silence is one silence. It was a glass table, I recall. I remember seeing the legs of my four interviewers. All emptiness one emptiness. Four pairs of trousers. Office clothes. I remember a sort of wonderment and bitterness that Julia had spoken to the Local Authority Allegations Committee – when? – yet had not been in touch with me. Had spoken and denied our love. Catherine is dead, I thought, and I am cut loose.

The one man at the table, spoke up. Mr Burrow, were

you aware that this relationship you say you had was causing distress to Mrs Ingram's children, who, given your position as headmaster, were in your care?

No. I answered emphatically. Absolutely not. Mrs Ingram always assured me her children knew nothing of our relationship. Since I have no teaching hours, I was not directly involved with them. I was completely unaware of any unease.

That was it. The investigation was over. Our relationship was over, surely. Likewise my time at the school.

It is with great regret, I wrote that same afternoon, that I have decided to resign my post, since I fear I will have lost the governors' trust.

'Eternal and maddening'

Back down the mountainside from Gurtnellen to the river Reuss. South up the valley to Wassen and Göschenen. Then onward through the Devil's Gorge to Andermatt, or perhaps directly over the mountain to the west, to Hospental, beneath the Gotthard. That will be my day. Except I'm late for breakfast. I turned off the alarm and fell asleep. Frau Bittli is irritated. The other guests have gone. She has begun to sweep the floor. Munching bread and jam, I study the map then glance through Lawrence's account of this day's walking. He took the easier route through the Devil's Gorge. *The narrow gulley of solid living rock*, he says. *The very throat of the path.* I've begun to feel more friendly towards Lawrence since we left Julia behind. The way men can be better friends, perhaps, when their women are not about. Though there is her underlining here and there. *It looks as though the industrial spread of mankind were a sort of dry disintegration* – USE! she scribbled in the margin – *advancing and advancing.* I'm more curious that he spoke of *living rock.* In what way living? I'll be a rock for you, I had told her. But all my life, I then reflect, seems to arrange itself into before Julia, during Julia and after Julia. And now this strange adventure, which is neither one nor the other. Or perhaps all three.

A man straddles a stool at the bar and Frau Bittli puts a bottle of Feldschlösschen in front of him. He didn't order anything that I heard. It's a routine. It's nine o'clock. More or less the hour the Feldschlösschen beer wagon would routinely drive by Grubenhof. Remarkably it was horse drawn. And without saying anything the driver would hand down a bottle to Gerhard. Sometimes two bottles. They were big black horses swishing their tails and clopping their hooves. Big brown bottles. Gerhard kept an opener on the windowsill of the cow stall and we leaned on our pitchforks and drank. The man at the bar is laughing with Frau Bittli. They're speaking dialect. It felt like a lot of fun to be drinking beer beside the dung heap at nine a.m. Gerhard was so jolly when the drink wet his lips. I was nineteen. He never made me pay.

Was macht das? I step up to the bar to settle my bill. The man turns to me. He's fortyish with shiny cheeks and small brown eyes. Brown teeth. He says something I can't understand. *Nein!* Frau Bittli rebukes him and wags a stern finger. She turns to me more indulgently now. The bill is as expected. *Herr Burrow*, she announces in a loud cheerful voice, *Gute Reise!* And she claps her hands.

The valley narrows. The path runs along the flank of the mountain, a drop of steep scree to the left, grey rock rising to the right. Granite by the looks. The only thing that's living about it are the plants sprouting from every crack. Ferns and lichens and mosses. Dewy cobwebs spun over shoots of ivy. Nature never fails to seize an opportunity. Now there's a saint in the cliff face, raising his hand in blessing behind dirty glass. Now a stretch of pine wood. You can see the broken branches on the trunks, where the knots form. At one point the path intersects a great pipe running straight up the steep slope. Thousands of feet. Thousands of gallons of icy water. Iron stairways take me down a crevasse to a chapel on a spur. Go easy with your knee. *I am the forsaken Mother from the dusty forest*, says the Gothic script beneath a red-robed Madonna staring out across the void. I think that's what it says. *Whoever comes to me with trust, I will pray for them.*

I stop here for a moment, looking at the little statue, then at the drop into the valley, the airy prospect of the peaks above. I realise I'm attracted to these devotional images. The more rugged and remote the places they appear, the more attractive I find them. But I could never go to them with trust. Margaret was the churchgoer. Perhaps what attracts me is the idea of trust. However misplaced.

The path winds its way down in rocky steps strewn with twigs and pinecones. I grasp the railing anchored to the cliff. After the drama comes the shame. Something had eluded me in the relationship between Julia and her daughter. I hadn't paid attention. You realise something decisive has happened – I bring my right leg down carefully where the left has gone first – and hence suppose that everything is over. I immediately understood our affair was over. But in reality it has only just begun. A turmoil that will go on unfolding for years. Had Julia denied our affair to protect me? Or to protect herself? Did she speak to the Local

Authority before going to the retreat? Or during. If before, why did they wait so long before speaking to me? Or perhaps it wasn't long, in their scheme of things. Did she lie to me about her family? Or did she honestly not realise her daughter knew? Did I ever really trust her? Or her me? I loved her vitality, yes, I loved her trust in herself, her strange obsession with a writer who had run off with a German woman. Lawrence was so sure of himself, she marvelled. A hundred years before. When he sent that famous letter. When he told a husband he was running off with his wife, the mother of their children, because they were in love. I was in love with Julia. Surely that was all that mattered. I loved her turbulence. Her eagerness to live. I never had the impression there was anything strange about her relationship with her children. Catherine Julia Ingram the letter was signed. If only we had told the truth, right at the beginning. A For Sale sign appeared in Grove Park Road. But you've only just bought the place, Rachel protested when she saw the For Sale sign in Oxford Road South. She brought along Steve that day; a quiet, bearded young man. She prepared a quiche for us all. He seemed in awe of me. He sat at the table as if sitting for an exam. When I bought this place, I said, I was having a relationship with a woman who was supposed to move in with me. With her children as well. But it fell through.

Do Not Stay In The Riverbed! A sign shows a fleeing figure chased by a huge blue wave. It's curling over his head. Hydroelectric plants can cause sudden flooding at any time. In fact, the Reuss is low and quiet here. Blue pools draining gently through white rocks. A couple of families are paddling with their children. There's a dog splashing about. I follow the railway for a while. I'm back on the official Gotthard path now. Swiss National Trail No.7. Persistent heavy rainfall caused the Reuss to swell disastrously in August 1987, says panel 18, destroying a hundred metres of rail track.

There is a pretty girl serving at the Hotel Gerig in Wassen. She moves lightly between the guests in black T-shirt and brown skirt. Two other hikers are sitting at the table opposite mine, an older man and a younger woman, with shiny trekking poles, smart packs. When they try to set up a selfie, the waitress offers to take the picture for them. It's the slyness of her mouth I find so alluring. She crouches on the steps pointing the man's phone. *The people catch a new tone*, Lawrence thought, *from their contact with the foreigners*. Move over a little, she gestures to the woman. She's bored with being a waitress in a godforsaken mountain village. She hands back the phone and lingers, chatting, but a voice calls her from the hotel. There's the whine of a vacuum cleaner. Her ordinary life. So where are you planning to move now? Rachel asked. She turned abruptly from the oven, from her quiche. There was never anything remotely sly about Rachel. Brittle rather. She wasn't married, I hope! This woman. Why didn't you tell me before? Because she was married, I said. Steve laughed. And I said, I'm going back to Yorkshire, Rach.

The cloud has lifted. Suddenly the sun is burning again, as it did in Konstanz and Eglisau. Drinking my coffee outside the Hotel Gerig, in the warmth and light, I feel oddly convalescent, as if I'd survived a tough illness. The couple stand up to leave. There really is quite an age difference between them. Twenty years. Thirty? But they seem so at ease with each other. They're wearing rings. She dabs suncream beneath his eyes. He cleans her glasses for her. You can see it's a routine they have. Packs on their backs, poles in their hands. She tries to straighten his hat. *Basta!* he cries. I hadn't realised they were Italian. They're laughing. Tears come to my eyes. You haven't survived anything is the truth. Twenty years on, you're still a sucker for a sly twist of the lips, still falling apart at the sight of a man and a woman in love. It was the fact that Catherine told the truth that was so devastating. In her letter. I didn't see that at the time. I was so relieved there were no false allegations. She hadn't taken advantage of those five minutes in my office to invent God knows what. As things stood, I'd done nothing illegal. There was nothing that could blot my record as teacher or headmaster. Only slowly did I see how Catherine's painful truth must spread across our story like a sort of dry disintegration. Everything rotted and shrivelled. Our pleasure was ugly and unthinkable.

But was it true that Julia was 'unable to escape from it'? Surely Catherine was lying there. Or deluding herself. You don't say anything for years, Rachel phoned. Then you come out with it just like that, in front of Steve as well. I like Steve, I said. He's your boyfriend, isn't he? That's not the point, she said. She said, You don't mean you're going to live in our old school again? Are you, Dad? The idea seemed to horrify her. The idea that Julia wanted to escape me is horrifying. I refuse to consider it. You know, I told my daughter, I only came to London because you were here. I'm just going to teach, I said. I won't be headmaster. There's a vacancy for geography. I'll live in the village. A few minutes later she phoned back. I'm sorry, Dad. Her voice was calmer. I didn't think. Think what? I asked. That you must be upset. She hesitated. Things must be bad if you've decided to go back. There was a long silence on the line. If there's anything I can do, she said. You'll be fine, in London, I told her. You're doing fine. I like Steve, I said. He reminds me of myself, when I was young.

And now this pretty waitress is reminding me of someone. I sit over my coffee longer than I meant to, trying to fathom it. Who? Is being reminded of people a talent or a curse? I watch her go on tiptoe to squeeze between two chairs. She's wearing white sneakers. I watch her lips pucker as she scribbles an order, brushes back her hair. Now she raises an eyebrow in my direction to ask if I'm done. And I have it. I get to my feet. Definitely a curse.

Beyond Wassen a man on a bench asks me where I'm going. The bench is facing away from the road to pastures and snowy heights, but the man turns exactly as I pass by, as though he'd heard my footsteps. Despite the traffic. Hospental, I tell him. He's an old man, in his seventies at least. He's missing teeth, has bloodshot eyes, but seems surprisingly vigorous, even belligerent. Why are you walking on the road? he demands. Perhaps he's drunk a beer or two. You can go to Hospental over the mountain. I have to ask him to repeat what he said. His speech is slurred. The views are much better that way, he says. The path is right there. He points behind me to a passage under the railway embankment. That's the way.

145

I try to explain that I'm tired. I slept badly, started late. I had thought of going over the mountain, but decided against.

Perhaps my German isn't clear. He shakes his head. I realise there's a scythe propped against the bench. He's been scything the steep bank beneath the road. He's been working in these mountains all his life. Much prettier up there, he repeats. Much better than walking on this horrible road. Go that way. He points to the passage under the railway. And I go.

Immediately the other side of the tracks, the path forks. It's a steep climb. A train passes below. It's a red, child's toy of a train. Just three carriages. Beyond the railway, beside the road, the old man is on his feet, sharpening his scythe. At Grubenhof the farmer's father always had a sharpening stone in his pocket. And a stub of cigar in his mouth, under a yellowing moustache. A stooped, slender man. Also in his seventies I suppose. It was impossible to speak to him. He didn't understand me and I could never make out a word he said. I never saw the cigar lit. His only activity was to scythe the steep edges of the fields where the motor mower couldn't go. He wore blue dungarees and a straw hat, moving stiffly, cutting just a few armfuls of grass at a time. Occasionally his son, the farmer, would make some ironic remark, passing by. Or perhaps he put an arm round his shoulders. The old man grunted. There was always a dribble of saliva at the corner of his mouth. Brown from the cigar. His time was over. He never ate with the rest of the family. I never thought of him. I haven't thought of him in forty years.

I haven't been climbing ten minutes when the path peters out in coarse meadow and brambles. Did I take the wrong turn at the fork? My map has too many fine lines. Some dotted, some solid, some red, some black. With the slope being so steep the lines seem to lie on top of each other. The arrowhead showing my position keeps jumping from side to side. Take it easy, I tell myself. I sit on a stone. I must get this right. The old man is still visible, on the slope beneath the road. Swaying slightly with his scythe. The mountain path will take me to seven thousand feet. Along a high ridge. It's not clear exactly where one comes down to Hospental.

And it's too hot. I sit staring across the valley. I had so much more energy yesterday, in the rain, the mist. Down on the autobahn, beside the river, the southbound traffic seems to have come to a standstill. A windscreen catches the sunlight. Something feels wrong. I walk back to where the paths forked. Three or four years after my stay at Grubenhof I received a message via my parents. Anouk's cousin had come to study in Manchester. Anouk had given her my home address. I was married by then and Margaret would have felt threatened by any mention of foreign girlfriends. I met Lena alone in a café on campus. A pretty smile and a bob of blonde hair. Much prettier than Anouk. Sparkling eyes. Bubbly conversation. We talked about Anouk and Grubenhof. How was everybody? I asked. The farmer, his wife, the girls. Gerhard?

Didn't you hear about Gerhard?

Back at the fork I study the map again. I think I've seen my mistake. The high trail is enticing. But I'm not going to go for it. It's too much. I head back under the railway line to the road, the busy road from Wassen to Göschenen. I'm in the same place I was half an hour ago. So is the old man. He's cut a little grass and is sitting on the bench again, his scythe beside him, looking away across the valley. He haunts this bench, it seems. Waylaying hikers. And what's infuriating is that I feel embarrassed. I am trying to sneak past this old peasant, praying that he doesn't turn round and ask me why I am not taking the route over the mountain, the pretty route, with the better views, as any real man would. The hero's route. Why have I fallen back on the dull road, with the dull crawl of industrial traffic up the valley? Why do you always fall back? The question doesn't seem to need a speaker. It's in the air. Why do you always try to sneak round people even when your decisions make perfect sense? You're so conservative. It made perfect sense to see Anouk's cousin Lena, yet I remember concocting some absurd excuse to sneak away from Margaret's watchful eye. Gerhard hung himself, Lena said. In the cowshed. Johanna found him. He drank a lot, you know. His wife was depressed. He had gambling debts. I keep to the other side of the road, by the railway embankment, fixing my eyes straight ahead, walking fast. If the old man turns, I won't see him. I don't understand how he managed to turn the first time, at exactly the moment I passed. In any event, I don't hear anyone calling after me and at two thirty I'm in the Göschenen Coop buying rolls and ham and apples and yoghurt.

Disorder and sterile chaos, high up, Lawrence says. *Railway sidings and haphazard villas for tourists.* This is the mouth of the Gotthard tunnels for rail and autobahn. It's true it's ugly. Most of the wounds which the construction of the railway inflicted on Nature are now healed, claims a panel beside the path. It doesn't feel like that. But it's an exciting ugliness. There's a strange excitement in Göschenen. I feel galvanised. All that motorised wilfulness racing into the dark. To burrow its way through miles and miles of rock. Renouncing the beauty above, the snow-topped crags, the white ribbons of falling water. Breathing nothing of the fresh air and the pine resin. Forgoing all intimacy with the damp earth and the clouds, the moss and the crocus and the silent high circling of the buzzards. There's something suicidal about flinging yourself into the dark of a tunnel. But you arrive more quickly.

My path crosses the Reuss again, all white boulders and rushing water now, then crosses back, as the valley narrows and winds and climbs and the old road climbs and winds with it, until I'm in a tight gorge of grey rock walls, the river beneath full of detritus, broken bridges, broken dams, abandoned projects of other times. Great blocks of stone are crashed on their sides, rusting iron rods driven into granite. You wanted a rock. I'm here. Touch me. Hide in me. Finally, the only place left for the path is above the shelter that projects from the cliff to protect the road from falling stones. It's a wide grass-covered track, grass over concrete, with the cars accelerating beneath your feet and the water tumbling all around. *Eternal and maddening*, Lawrence says. *Rustling and rushing and wavering, but never for a second ceasing.*

I keep up a steady pace through the Devil's Gorge. The

questioning never ceased in the first months back in York-shire. It was maddening to wake every morning and every morning be back on Lake Lucerne, back in Altdorf. To hear a shriek in the dead of night and ride a taxi through the dawn. And amid all this unhappiness, one question that gradually gathered weight and mass until it crashed down like an avalanche. I was walking home from school. It caught me with my key in the door. Why didn't you insist on seeing her? Why? Why did you accept at once that the daughter was right, was telling the truth? Just because she died. I knew immediately it was a question that would come at me a thousand times, like headlights in a tunnel. Why not make one brave attempt to wrest Julia from this sadness and self-harm, to pit our happiness against her daughter's destiny? Why not say, Julia, despite all that's happened, we can be happy? We can. It wasn't true she wanted to escape me. It wasn't true. Instead, you buried yourself in your old haunt, your old school. Cooking gloomy dinners alone. As if you had some sin to expiate. And in the months and years to come, but I already knew this would happen, you let the question wear itself out unanswered. One day a little louder, one day a little qui-eter, until at last its energy faltered, it began to seem quaint, outlandish, ridiculous. All the while teaching class after adolescent class about tectonic shifts and the accretion of fluvial sediments. The importance of access to the sea. Why had I never really tried to see Julia? Or she me?

It's bewildering how twisted and tangled this gorge is. The old road leaps over the void on a stone bridge while a local train shoots out of a tunnel across a viaduct above.

High in a narrow cleft three tiny figures are just visible from the yellow of their helmets, the red of a rope. The rock face is cracked and foliated, dark with patches of scrub, pink with foxgloves. There are gun emplacements. Storage caves. Now a wild, wild waterfall. The whole river plunges past the ledge where I stand. Impetuous beyond all reason. Far below a green pool awaits, calm in the deep shadow of the gorge, the very throat of the path. I feel glad I came this way. The rock may not be living but the place makes you feel alive. I feel glad people have hacked and tunnelled their way through here since time immemorial. At another twist of the path, walking beneath the road now, you can see a tall stone cross, thirty feet high, carved into the mountainside. General Suvorov led allied Russian and Austrian forces against the French. So a panel tells me. 25 September 1799. They captured the Devil's Bridge, an elegant arch in the midst of geological chaos. Still standing. The daring of it all is breathtaking. Hundreds of men died. When I reach the monument, Swiss and Russian flags are flying. There's a small space a hundred yards up the road where cars can park. Even a restaurant. Suddenly there are people. I'm in company again. Holiday families stretching their legs. A group of cyclists. Couples reading the information panels. Who would have thought the Russians fought here? Selfies by the grand inscription in gold Cyrillic letters, between two swords of stone. Incomprehensible and dramatic. A man is hawking sandwiches and Coke. I knew it was company that would get me through. In Yorkshire. All those children's faces. Year 8, Year 9, Year 10. Their noise and their smells. Their anxieties. I deliberately chose to teach. I would not have taken the headmaster's job if they'd begged me. I did not want responsibility. I wanted to annul myself in the war of attrition that teaching is. The noose over the beam was beyond me. The dive under the train. Likewise the charge and the bayonet. I wanted the daily struggle to keep the class quiet, the battle to drum a few basic facts into distracted minds. And the field trips. The White Scar Caves. The moors, the Peak District. Robin Hood Bay. There were always exams to plan, homework to mark. The more the better. Soon enough Julia would fade, Switzerland would fade.

A coach is unloading a hoard of ten-year-olds. Boys and girls dashing to the parapet to look down into the gorge. Some holding hands. I push on up the path. Another twenty minutes of steps and ledges and bridges and I'm out on open moorland, at four thousand feet, with the hotels and cranes of Andermatt just half a mile ahead, beneath another line of mountains. The climb has cheered me up. I feel pleased with myself. Convalescent again. Yet sometimes in the dead of night the strangest trains of thought would impose themselves. Catherine hadn't killed herself. Why had I been so quick to think that? It was an accident. She was drugged, drunk. No one else had spoken of suicide. And she hadn't known of our affair until the day she wrote that letter, under pressure from her father. Or rather, when she saw her father so upset, so angry – some confidant of Julia's had blabbed – she offered to write the letter for him. An entirely false letter. The husband's revenge against the lover. And when at last, years afterwards, Julia discovers this, she calls me, she weeps, she apologises. Why didn't we keep talking to each other? Why did we allow this to happen? We mustn't throw our love away. There was no end to these stories, with their twists and turns, their crevasses and fault lines, no end to the energy of this unfolding. Above all at night. When I lay awake at night. But once I got to sleep the recurrent dream was always Margaret, Margaret alive again, yet still dead. An atmosphere of anxiety and weariness. Awake, I never thought of Margaret at all. Not even at the school where we had lived together. It seemed physiological. I couldn't think of Margaret. I couldn't not think of Julia. Who never appeared in my dreams. The following year I became a grandfather.

A livid desolate waste, Lawrence thought. *Straggling and inconclusive. As if great pieces of furniture had tumbled out of a removal van.* Which sounds more like a description of my life than the place I find myself in, the picturesque main street of Andermatt. It's true there are modern ski-resort hotels, on the edge of town. But here everything is almost too neat. Too clean. At the bottom of a fairy-tale facade, pink, green and gold, is an inscription: *Quartier des Generalissimus SUWOROF, am 25. September 1799.* The window of the Tourist Information Office is advertising a yodelling festival. I eat an ice cream and walk on, past the guesthouses and the big car parks and the ski-lifts, into the open plain to the west that leads to Hospental. It's a flat valley floor here, with shallow slopes each side. None of the ski-lifts seem to be working. There are green fields beside the river but the slopes are a dull purple grey, strewn with rocks. *Nothing but winter's broken detritus*, Lawrence thought. I remember a skiing holiday was the first out-come of my discovery of online dating. In my fifties. Through the winter I would chat at the keyboard with three or four possible candidates. Always women far away. Preferably abroad. Preferably foreign. Eventually a meeting would be arranged. Since there was serious travel involved it would have to be for a few days. Three was the norm. So intimacy was expected without quite being inevitable. Skiing seemed the kind of activity one might use to move closer to someone and be sure of a decent weekend whatever the outcome. I remember Patrizia in Val Gardena. Leah in Bankso. Professional, divorced women, my age or a little younger. Ulrike in Tignes. The algorithm is fairly restrictive. I avoided mothers. A couple of widows. Summer trips too, once I'd got into the habit, sightseeing in famous cities. At the very least you would discover somewhere new. Buenos Aires the furthest afield, where Jazmin took me to a five-star bedroom with thirty red roses arranged in a heart on the white duvet. We only made love once. Only one of these little breaks was repeated. Once. Which didn't mean there wasn't some feeling and some fun. On return I made a habit of stopping in London to see my grandchildren, before the train to York, the bus to Malton. I remember Rachel would frown and ask me where I'd been. She has filled out. I showed her photos I'd selected on the plane. Her boys are charming. Beginning the new term, I braced myself for the inevitable depression. I signed up to dinner duty and blew the whistle on icy games of hockey. Dan always taught with passion, said the young headmaster at my retirement bash.

How weird, then, to find that the place I've booked, in Hospental, is officially a *Jugendherberge*. I hadn't realised. I hope my age isn't a problem, I say to the proprietor. He's a lean, stooping, wry man, trapped in a cubby-hole office. He shakes his head and takes me to a room I am to share with five others.

'The kingdom of the world had no significance'

Why am I here, on this ridge of the Alps, in the lamp-lit, wooden, close-shut room, alone? Why am I here?

Such were Lawrence's thoughts as he settled down in *the little village with the broken castle that stands forever frozen at the point where the path parts.*

I'm not alone in the *Jugendherberge*, but it's hard not to wonder why on earth I'm here. The dining room is packed. Adolescents. Families. Hikers and bikers. Helping themselves from the buffet. Salad, potatoes, veg, meat. Abundant. Tasty. I'm the only person over sixty, perched on the corner of a table packed with young men, shoulder to shoulder on rickety wooden benches. They have the lean faces and the birdlike torsos of racing cyclists. Everyone is talking, calling across the room. In German, French and Italian. Shoes are not allowed. People in bare feet or wearing trekking socks. I keep myself to myself, studying the photos on the wall, all peaks and snowscapes, then head for the bathroom early. There's a heap of climbing gear in the corridor. Girls in bathrobes on the stairs. Peals of laughter. Wet hair. Boys in their underpants. Everything is slippy and steamy. I am here of course because she sent me eighteen sheets of paper, thirty-six pages, torn from an old book. And she sent me these pages, it comes to me now, because there was nothing else.

Cleaning my teeth in the Jugendherberge Hospental, at 4,500 feet, my face in the mirror between two others, I'm astonished to recognise this new thought. There was nothing else. Was that what she wanted to say? Was this why we hadn't tried to contact each other afterwards? The boy to my right glares at himself as he shaves. As if at an implacable enemy. I stumble up the stairs, to the second floor, the third, then back to the bathroom to recover my toothpaste. Fortunately I have a lower bunk. I've slid my pack underneath. In what sense was there nothing else? I keep my phone beside me, with its torch, in case I have to get up in the night. She had this role model. Call him that. Lawrence. A man and a woman ran away together, lived a great love, in defiance of family and society. Became celebrities. She was wrapped up in her studies. Her denunciations of ordinariness. Of industrialised uniformity. She needed to do something dangerous. To emulate her heroes. I was that something. But at the same time I was safe, I was institutional, I was pliant.

I'm so fed up of thinking about this. But fascinated to see the story take a new turn. After all these years. A wiry young man has opened the window and lit a cigarette. The mountain air is chill. Another is examining his feet, legs swinging from the top bunk opposite mine. Behind it all, Lawrence. Nothing else. This writer I could never get interested in. And when there were no more obstacles and

157

the moment came for us to declare ourselves, what did we do? Did we move into the house I had prepared for her? The logical thing. No. We ran off after D. H. Lawrence. Into a sort of limbo. A honeymoon on the roof of the world. The roof of a department store. Waiting for catastrophe.

The man opposite has swung up his legs and is reading something on his phone. I'm enjoying the whiffs of tobacco from the window. Now a boy comes in, a teenager. But immediately a voice calls him back to the corridor. A soft French voice. He empties his pack on the floor and goes out carrying a phone charger. I could chuck these pages of Lawrence and say the hell with the whole thing. But I'm drawn to the man's restlessness. To the thought that even as she was dying, she sent me these pages. She thought of me. *I was free*, he writes, *in this heavy, ice-cold air, this upper world. London, far away below, beyond, England, Germany, France—they were all so unreal in the night.*

Another man comes in. He has the bottom bunk opposite mine. The man up top is his friend. They speak in low voices, in German, while the new arrival undresses. Do you have any water? What time should we set the alarm? I'm impressed by their easiness with all this intimacy. The soiled clothes, bare flesh. I'm hoping perhaps the bunk above mine will be left unoccupied. The smoker asks if we want the window open or closed. In German again. For sure Yorkshire, Malton, the classroom do seem far away. Below and beyond, as Lawrence says. Perhaps reality is simply where you are now, right now. Window open is the general verdict, but with the curtains drawn. Or nothing is real. Certainly the idea of Julia moving into Oxford Road

South with Catherine and John, should they so desire, always had something fantastical about it.

It was a sort of grief that this continent all beneath was so unreal, false, non-existent in its activity. My bunk is against the wooden wall and trembles as heavy feet pound the stairs outside. Voices call from landing to landing. Woman to man. Man to woman. They seem oddly familiar. A tall heavy figure bursts into the room. Hullo all! He sizes up the situation. So which bed is mine? A strong Yorkshire accent. As his heavy feet slap on the rungs beside me and the bunk trembles and creaks it's impossible to deny his reality. Now he climbs down again. Sorry, mate, toilet. No worries, I tell him. My accent attracts his attention. Finally he sees me. He's puzzled. Gasthaus Bergheim, I remind him. Last night. Oh right! He smiles. Good on you. He has a fleshy Tigger-ish smile. Why didn't you say you were English!

Everybody is on their beds now. Sending last texts. The French boy is wearing a headset, watching a video. *Out of the silence one looked down on it,* Lawrence winds up his day, *and it seemed to have lost all importance, all significance. It was so big, yet it had no significance. The kingdom of the world had no significance: what could one do but wander about?*

So what did you get up to today? The Yorkshireman is back. Sorry, fellas. He lowers his voice. Want me to get the light?

Yes, thank you. The German opposite rolls over to the wall.

I wandered here, I tell him, from the Gasthaus.

Right. Which way?

The Devil's Gorge.

How was it?

Interesting.

Close to the road, though, right?

Fraid so. And yourselves?

Came over the Spitzberg. Fucking stunning, I'm telling you, but took for ever. Glenda was whacked out. He chuckled. Thought I'd have to carry her at the end.

Everyone has settled but the French boy. His video throws shifting colours across the pine panelling, with its grains and knots. Julia is dead. And Catherine. And Margaret. Gerhard is dead. My working life is over. From time to time I checked Julia's career on the internet. Academic articles. *Intimations of Buddhism in D. H. Lawrence.* A postgrad course on Feminist Criticism. Then she was Dean of Faculty. But more and more rarely. Then not at all. *The kingdom of the world had no significance.* I like that. I like the thought of being beyond struggle and competition. As when you watched the children doing their exams. Or competing for a place in the team. Glad you were not them. How happy, I realise, the big Yorkshire boy had been to say his girlfriend was whacked out. His rather superior girlfriend. You underrate yourself, Margaret would say. Apply to be headmaster. Go for it. Go for the prize, she told Rachel. Your drawings are the best. An ambitious man has no time for other women. Was that the logic? Certainly Julia was ambitious.

The big boy above me turns and the bunk shudders and creaks. Comes a faint snore. From outside a distant splash of water over stones. Faint sounds mingling in the dark. *What can one do but wander about?* No doubt that was another reason for this trip: to delay the decision, what to do after retirement.

Are the others asleep? I'm enjoying my wakefulness tonight. It's rare to share a room with strangers. I'm enjoying the thought that these young men are all busy with their lives, their girlfriends, their jobs. While I'm beyond. I remember my young self centuries ago, reaching from one couchette to another to touch a girl's hand. It's funny, of all the things you do, those that remain. Our fingers twined a while, then slid apart. What if we had held on? What if Julia and I had kept on walking, here to Hospental. And over the Gotthard. To Italy. I did love her. I would have kept my promises. I can't imagine what it would have been like, but I know that was what I wanted. They could have thrown me out of school, destroyed my reputation. I wouldn't have cared.

Swinging my legs out of the bunk towards dawn I'm sour and angry. Was there some dream? Was it fondness made her send those pages? Or whim? The torch on the phone gets me through the clutter to the door. There's a nightlight on the stairs. We lost a struggle, Julia and I, that's the truth of the matter. Father and daughter versus mother and lover. Stakes raised beyond all expectation. A stainless-steel urinal runs the length of the wall. I watch my pee slide away over the shiny surface. Did it need to end so dramatically? Very likely a little hoo-ha would have been enough. Climbing the stairs, I try to remember the two that creak. Julia's values were not Lawrence's values. The kingdom of the world kept all its significance for her. One bloodcurdling scream and our wandering was over.

'This upper, transcendent desolation'

Where to now? Today I'm going to think about the future. In the centre of Hospental stands a broken tower. Squat grey stone silhouetted in the dawn light. I'm the first out of the hostel. There's a bright orange mould on the rocks in the Reuss. The river flows from the west, but my path leads south. A tight little valley with a bubbly stream. Rocks and scrub and willowherb. I think it's willowherb. Spearheads of pink flowers. The road is high up on the slope to my right. Deserted at this hour. At this hour you can enjoy the silence. The moorland smells. Sun tipping the peaks, shadow all around. Dark clumps of bog pine. And a clang of cow bells. Sleek grey animals tug at coarse grass between the stones. I climb steadily, with a new feeling of satisfaction. I'm going to think about the future. In fact, I don't think anything at all.

After an hour or so, a tiny stone bridge crosses the stream. It's a beautiful path. Carefully signed. Ahead, the slope rises more steeply towards the pass. Looking back, the valley is wonderfully bleak. There are a few cars up on the road now, but I can barely hear them. Far away, where the stream drops down to Hospental, I spy two figures, side by side. I watch them a moment, climbing the path after me through the stony scree. One has a red cap. They seem to be moving quite fast.

Where to live? What to do with one's time? The big questions are always the same. The novelty is not needing to earn. Someone has pitched a small blue tent high up on the slope to my left. A nomad. I lack a centre of gravity, I know that. Something to orbit around. Sediments that failed to compact, washed away downstream years ago. The old grandfather at Grubenhof never asked these questions. First he was his father's helper, then the main man, then his son's helper, scything the grass on the margins of the farm. Planet home. Cigar long dead but still in his mouth. A dead knot in the pine cladding of Grubenhof. The word *Planetenweg* came to mind. Would you like to reach for the stars? Incredible I remember Julia reading those words. Incredible that she wept on my chest and begged me to be strong for her. No notion of the black hole that would draw her back. Gravity is something people do together perhaps.

The sun is creeping down the mountain as I climb towards it. I'm not looking forward to its heat. The walkers behind me are closer too. It's the Yorkshire couple. Stopping to drink, I can see their arms swinging as they advance. Perhaps I should have fought to stay on, at school. It was always the nearest thing to home. I paid more attention to the problems of my pupils than to relations in the Ingram household. Geography is about getting your bearings in the world, I would tell them. Where you are is who you are. Your position in relation to the rest. I have to smile, thinking of this now. In this waste of rocks and ferns. It should have been the husband confronting me, not the daughter. *This upper, transcendent desolation.* And I should have told him the truth, face to face. All around broken stones and purplish moor grass. Julia was mad to think she could emulate Lawrence. She was miles out of her comfort zone. Always a passionate teacher, the young headmaster commended me. But he was adamant that none of us stay on beyond retirement age. Paying parents want to see new blood. They want energy and inclusiveness. I thought, If it isn't this year, it will be next.

I can hear their voices now, both raised. You're joking! She is shrill. Never more serious, he protests. I wait beside the path to let them go by. I'm happy to rest. They come marching up. Him with his red baseball cap. Look who it isn't, he cries. Someone got up early! He pulls a water bottle from his girlfriend's pack and stops to drink. Are you from Yorkshire? Her face is plump and round, flushed with exertion. Her eyes sparkle. Not guilty, I tell her. But I've lived there a while. We're from Leeds, she says. Want to walk with us? I'm Glenda. Pete. The boy offers his hand. I'm afraid you're much faster than me, I tell them.

Well, speed up then! Pete laughs.

We can slow down, Glenda says. A bit. She laughs and drinks and wipes her mouth on her wrist.

Anyone want a biscuit? The boy turns so that his girlfriend can open his pack. I'm Dan, I tell them.

The path has climbed above the road now as the valley widens and flattens. A couple of camper vans are parked beside a small lake. It's hard work marching with these youngsters. But not impossible. They stop from time to time to let me catch up, almost as if I were their child. Wagtail! Glenda cries. See? She points to the sky. Have you seen any eagles? she asks. We're collecting a list of butterflies, Pete says solemnly. Yesterday we saw a queen of Spain. It was never a queen of Spain, Glenda sighs. I have the photo, he protests. Know what that is? He points to a curious concrete pavilion on the slope beyond the stream. Tunnel ventilation. We're walking over the autobahn, aren't we?

They are constantly noticing things. Beetles, birds, flowers. It's a competition. A gentian! That's never a gentian. What is it, then?

I can't join in. I'm thinking of the road rushing beneath us. The tug of the road. The cars locked together in their speed. Pure wilfulness. The slow lane, the fast. It's pretty weird, Julia would say, your not driving. You should really get a licence. You're always telling me I'm too conventional, I laughed. But all at once I'm thinking of the woman in Jestetten. Heike. Why did she imagine I left an umbrella when I didn't bring one? Do women mother me because I can't drive?

Need a break? Glenda calls.

I'm fine.

They wait while I catch up. The slope has eased. Pete complains about a giant pylon slinging a dozen cables over a ridge. An eyesore. Nothing's sacred, he grumbles. We're walking across a sort of shallow bowl of bog and stray boulders and patches of water. It's miles across. Around the edges, wind turbines stand forlorn in the day's stillness. The wires have to go somewhere, Glenda says. In

1913 Lawrence complained that soldiers were using the pass for shooting practice. But I don't want to talk to them about Lawrence. I feel a little let down by the place, frankly. It seems more sad than special. They could put the wires underground, Pete insists, with the motorway. But now a stone beside the path tells us we're passing from Canton Uri to Canton Ticino and the boy does a little jig and throws his arms wide and sings, ITALIA! Italian Switzerland, Glenda corrects. But they speak Italian, Pete objects and abruptly he asks me, What do you do, Dan?

Retired.

But what did you do?

I can't see any way out. Geography teacher.

No! Glenda is delighted. Quiz, she says. We gotta have a quiz! What states border with Canton Ticino? Main towns and rivers. Highest peak in the Gotthard Massif, Pete chips in. Then he asks, What school, where? And when I tell him he objects, But isn't that private?

It is.

There's a brief silence. Then Pete begins to say he couldn't teach in a private school. Ever. He teaches Biology. He's so fed up. But at least he's helping ordinary kids. When I'm really down, I tell myself, at least I'm doing something useful.

Rich kids are children too, Glenda observes. I ask her what she does. Young People's Mental Health Services, she recites. Leeds County Council. Basically, I try to stop teenagers killing each other. Or themselves.

But really, Pete seems quite worked up, how could you work in a private school? You don't seem the type.

I suppose there was a job available and I applied for it. It was years ago. After a big comprehensive in Manchester it felt like a good environment to be working in.

But teachers should be proactive. Don't you think? We should be working to make a better world, not pandering to the enemy. If you—

For Christ's sake, Peter, don't get on your high horse, Glenda snaps.

Oddly it's only when she pronounces his full name that I realise it's the same as Julia's husband's.

You work with poor kids, he turns to her. You wouldn't waste time with rich kids and their eating disorders.

Maybe I should, she bristles. Maybe I will. She starts to talk about her work. She sees too many children. Adolescents. There is too much bureaucracy. People are overwhelmed, alcoholic, ignorant, suicidal, violent. And drugged. Last week a boy pulled a knife. A girl spat at her. You can see why therapists dream of opening a private practice and seeing a half-dozen civilised anorexics.

You do a great job, Pete protests.

None of us wants to die a hero, she complains. What do you think, Dan?

I think we've arrived, I announce. It's coffee time.

We've reached the pass. There's a reedy lake and a scatter of modern buildings. A statue on a pile of stones, a car park, food stands. Everything is rough and raw. Coarse grass, whitish stones. Someone is barbecuing sausages. An ice-cream van pumps fumes. We sit at a rickety table on the bare rock of the massif and watch a squadron of bikers file by. I offer coffee and cake all round. Apricot cake.

Prices are exorbitant. Pete takes two pieces. The conversation turns to our trip. I'm walking down to Como, I explain. Which should take about three days from here. No particular reason. Just the excitement of crossing from north to south. And no, if there's one thing I never am, it's lonely. I have my thoughts, I tell them, to keep me company. I'm enjoying playing the older, wiser man.

You're not going down by the road, though?

Trail 7. I've booked a room in Airolo.

Pete shakes his head. Trail 7 is never more than a few yards from the road. We've checked it on Google Earth. The descent on the southern side is narrower and steeper. They just send you down with the traffic. More or less. What's the point of coming up here if you're always breathing fumes?

Come with us, Glenda cries.

They're going to climb the Pizzo Centrale. The highest peak hereabouts. Another three thousand feet. Then skirt the valley to the east and drop right down over Airolo where the train comes out of the tunnel. Tomorrow morning they'll buy a ticket to Florence.

Will we be in Airolo by nightfall?

Should be. Or not long after.

Come on, do it! Glenda urges. Let's climb!

It's eleven o'clockish. We've made good time.

I'll have to buy some sandwiches, I tell them.

Edelweiss

Why do this young couple want me tagging along? I wonder. I can only be a drag on them. But why did I agree to come?

The path climbs east above a shallow lake where two men are racing remote-controlled boats. Pathetic, is Pete's verdict. They're model gunboats, wobbling on the water a yard or so apart while their owners cheer them on.

Why do you always have to be Mr Hypercritical? Glenda asks.

Maybe because I see idiocy all around me. What do you think?

I have to concentrate on keeping up with them. It's actually a road rather than a path. Barely wide enough for a single vehicle. Three cyclists overtake us, one pulling a trailer with camping gear. You can see the muscles straining in his calves. I'm in a sweat already. Pete and Glenda discuss whether they should try cycling next year. You could cover so much more territory, Pete says. He starts to tell me about his problems at school. Being the youngest recruit, they've given him classes no one else wants, where results are poorest. He's absolutely determined to help the kids, he has great relationships with them as a rule, only most of these don't want to be helped. Then the head judges you on the basis of their exam achievement. It's ridiculous. How can I compete with a teacher teaching the A stream?

It's not a competition! Glenda cries.

Try telling that to the stupid head, Pete objects.

After a short silence, Glenda asks me, What do you think, Dan?

We're skirting a steep slope to our left; the valley to our right is thick with vegetation, rhubarb leaves it looks like, with three or four streams tumbling down to the pass.

Oh, I sympathise, I tell them. Teaching is a long haul. In the end you do what you can.

This platitude seems to smooth the waters. Glenda takes a photo of some white and yellow flowers. Are they heartsease? she wonders. I recall that Julia told me Lawrence had been a schoolteacher, in London, but gave up because of his ill health. He was fit enough to hike thirty mountain miles a day, but too frail to teach. Perhaps Pete would be cheered to hear that. But I have no desire to mention Lawrence. I'm glad to have turned my back on him. Why should a dead writer decide my route? Or conversation. It's never clear in those pages why he was taking that walk. You feel there must have been something else, some trouble he was fleeing from. Or fleeing towards. And Julia didn't give a damn about ecocriticism except as bait for funding. Everything about our Swiss adventure was false. We never knew where we were going is the truth. Or why.

Look, Pete cries. The Pizzo.

The road has flattened. A fork to the right crosses the valley and climbs the spur of the mountain southwards. Directly ahead is a great grey concrete wall. It can only be a dam. Above and behind, barren slopes rise sharply to grim crags, high in a blue sky.

Woo hoo! Glenda yells. Ten thousand feet here we come!

A hairpin brings us up to the level of the dam. Picnickers are sitting beside a narrow lake. A couple of men fishing. The water follows the curve of the valley to the right. We strike up to the left. In single file on a stony path. Pete leads the way. The steeper the slope the more he seems to accelerate. Glenda strides gamely after. They asked me, I realise, precisely because I'll be a drag on them. They have someone to look after.

No one talks now. We're exposed on the stony slope under a hot sun. What grass there is is dull and coarse. It lies flat on the hard ground. Glenda is a few yards up ahead. A strong stocky woman in blue shirt and shorts. Pete is out of sight. Do people make these choices consciously? I wonder. Surely they can't have said in so many words, We won't fight so much between ourselves with this old bloke in tow. And I didn't think, Agreeing to go with these youngsters I can finally turn my back on Lawrence. On the whole sad story of our Swiss walk. Change the narrative. But that must have been the reason. I can hardly run off with my children's headmaster. Julia did say that. Julia actually wrote that to me. Those very words. So she *was* conscious. But did she know that was *why* she chose me? Because it was impossible. And me? For years we lamented the obstacle that kept our affair clandestine. Isolated us in our passion. Stopped us growing. An obstacle we had chosen. Invented even. Would the world have ended if we had declared ourselves? Would anyone have died, or even been fired, if we had acted boldly, told the truth? Then when the obstacle was no longer there, we were lost, disorientated. Like someone trying to use a compass that is only a tattoo. The obstacle had been our centre of gravity.

Water is splashing down the rock face and across the path. Pete and Glenda are waiting for me. Three slabs serve as stepping stones across a transparent pool. Pete has filled his baseball cap and spills the water over his head. It runs down his bull neck. Sexy! he shivers. Glenda is crouched with her hands and forearms in the stream, assuming an ecstatic smile. These two love to make an exhibition of their pleasures.

Does Geography Teacher know what rock it is? Pete asks.

I stare through the thin curtain of falling water where the surface is clean, grey, finely grained.

Some kind of amphibolite? With metamorphics, identity is always a bit of a hotchpotch.

Ready? Glenda asks.

There's less grass now. No pasture. More stone and rubble and scree. All grey. Not just on our slope but across the panorama opening up all around. The peaks that seemed so magical from a distance are stony waste close up. I'm breathing hard, picking my way along a thread of a path beside a sheer drop. Far below, the lake is a speck of blue. God, am I hot! Glenda shouts. That's why I love you, Pete calls from up ahead. I focus on where to put my feet, scrambling up a gulley now, how to shift my weight, which stones are safe and which might move, using my hands here and there to steady myself. I mustn't slip. Emerging at the top, a wide boulder field opens up, rising steadily a couple of hundred yards towards the next cliff face, apparently impenetrable. You have to trust that there will be a way through. Medium difficulty, the Swiss hiking app says.

Right in the middle of this avalanche of stones there's something red. A red figure, it looks like. How strange. Maybe five feet high. Painted on a bank of rock. A girl. Pinkish red with a blank grey face. I stop for a breather and clean my sunglasses on my shirt. The figure stands upright but tilted to the left with the tilt of the rock, as if the mountain had moved after she was painted.

Glenda has climbed on a boulder to make a video of the view, turning 180 degrees, from Pete almost at the cliff to me coming out of the gulley.

Weird, I tell her. Someone painting a girl up here.

Right, she says distractedly.

The figure seems to be wearing a red hood, or a red cloak with a pointed hood, and is outlined in a band of white. Munch's *Scream* it could be.

Maybe someone died, she suggests, climbing down from her boulder.

But there's nowhere to fall.

Glenda looks around. Lightning? Hey, Pete! she calls. Did you see this weird thing on the rock?

What's that?

This weird girl someone's drawn.

He works his way back to us and clambers down beside the bank of rock and the pink figure, then bursts out laughing. He puts his meaty hands on his hips and guffaws theatrically.

Glenda frowns, on her guard.

I can't believe it, he roars. He doubles up. He really is a hefty presence.

What? Glenda shouts.

A girl? A girl! What's wrong with you?

We're perplexed.

He turns off the laughter and smiles. Come on now, children, I'll give you a little clue. Let me see . . . red, right? The colour red, yes? And, hmm, white. Are you following? Red and white, in combination with, hmm, mountain paths.

Immensely pleased with himself he makes pulling gestures with his hands as if trying to draw an intelligent word from our dumb mouths.

It's a fuckin' arrow, in't it! he cries. A huge big fat arrow. How do you think I found my way across all these stupid rocks?

Glenda groans. Dan said, Look at the girl and I saw a girl.

Girls on the brain, mate, Pete mocks me. You're a dark one.

But what about the face? I'm bemused. Doesn't it look like a face under a pointy hood?

He goes close and rubs his finger on the rock. It's the grey of the stone, isn't it, where some paint's come off.

Normally the path signs are small horizontal flashes, Glenda defends herself.

Normally there's a path to follow, not a great ocean of bloody boulders to scramble over.

Trudging on, the image stays in my mind. Pete's right, of course. But it's still the figure of a girl, I remember. Exposed on the mountainside. Pink in the greyness. Tipped to one side by some geological convulsion. A stone slithers beneath my boot. Don't go there, I tell myself. Concentrate.

We're climbing through scree now. Higher and higher. The stones are smaller, looser, blacker. The path is punishingly steep and my heart is thumping. Glenda humming something. Ankles and calves ache and strain. I don't think I've ever climbed to ten thousand feet. On the ridge above, a line of sharp crags are shaft-like, vertical, menacing. Pagan idols guarding the summit. Don't say that to Pete. Edelweiss! he yells. The big boy has found a white flower. Glenda hurries to take a photo. Immediately the two of them are bellowing at the top of their voices into the empty air: Edelweiss, edelweiss, every morning you greet me! They're still at it when I catch up. Hidden in a cranny, the lone flower looks scrawny, long-suffering. Join in! Glenda demands. Come on! And I do. The three of us arm in arm, facing out over the immensity of the landscape, singing: Blossom of snow may you bloom and grow! They have strong voices. I'm growing to like them. It's crazy to imagine I was responsible for Catherine's death. Glenda even throws in a harmony on the final line. Bless my homeland forever. I'm overwhelmed. By a soppy song. From that moment I know what's going to happen. I can't stop it. In a way it's already happening. We reach the summit and I burst into tears.

A pyramid of weathered rubble, rising from a long grey ridge. Patches of the same orange mould I saw on the stones in the Reuss at Hospental. On the very top, a dozen slabs have been raised in a pile to mark the spot. You can turn 360 degrees, the whole world is beneath you, a chaos of empty rock, grey fading to blue in a wash of warm air. Countless peaks and valleys, still and silent as far as the eye can see. Rags of snow in the hollows. The faintest breeze. The thought comes to me: Is this the mirage we saw that morning from Felsenegg? When we gazed at the mountains from the closed café. At once I'm sobbing. I have to sit on the stones. I shake my head. No it's nothing. Bit of emotion from the climb. My chest is heaving. Sorry. Can't help myself.

The two youngsters are respectful. They move off and try to name the distant peaks from the maps on their phones. Glenda complains she's not getting a signal. Later, eating our sandwiches with our backs to a rock, I sense they're rather pleased with my little performance. They enjoyed the drama. It adds to their sense of achievement. Someone else is in trouble. But let that be the end of it, I tell myself firmly. This trip is over as far as I'm concerned. Pete consults his watch. We need to get moving, he says.

I-spy

The descent is more painful than the climb. But I knew that would be the case. It's not difficult, but relentless. Down down down. I press myself against a wall of rock. Every step has to be placed with care. Twist an ankle and you'll be here for hours. My knee starts to complain. I have to go first with the left leg, then bring the right to the same place. It's slow going. The valley floor seems impossibly far away. I'm further and further behind. The youngsters stop and wait. I can hear them laughing and joking. Arguing over the words of a song. As soon as I arrive they're off again. After an hour or so my thigh muscles begin to tremble. I feel dizzy. Keep drinking. At least I brought plenty of water. At least I can't think about anything else but the next step. Where on earth did this business of responsibility come from? A girl on the rock. Blank face, like the Madonna beside the stream leaving Gurtnellen. You know it's a face but it has no features.

Finally, we're back beside the lake, back in the lazy hum of an ordinary summer afternoon. Children rushing in and out of the water. I'm so relieved. My legs are wobbly but I'm okay. I say I'm okay. Pete shares round a slab of almond cake. Waves away a wasp. He seems more adult now. The big man in charge of the expedition. The strong one. It's almost four thirty. So, he explains, now we head south a ways, where the road forks beyond the dam. Remember? Following the Ticino, but high up. That way we avoid going back to the Gotthard and the main road down the gorge. Then we drop into the valley just before Airolo. His app has a path, he says. It's a serious app. He has paid for the professional version. If he gives up teaching he'd like to be a mountain guide.

How far down is it?

No idea.

Since we're all still munching cake, I consult my phone. The battery is low. I remember I kept it by the bed last night instead of charging it. I imagined I'd be on Trail 7 with its endless signs and info panels. Home and dry by early afternoon.

Airolo is 1,175 metres, Glenda beats me to it. According to Wiki. About four thousand feet. We're around seven here.

And we've come down from ten.

Right.

Plenty of time to recuperate before we hit the descent, Pete says.

We cross the dam. There's a narrow walkway with railings either side. To the left the lake with its countless tons of icy water. To the right, a hundred feet below, the dry valley, its stream reduced to a trickle. Somewhere there must be turbines. There must be a reason for damming this water. But I can't see them. Along the road we walk three abreast, Glenda in the middle. They've slowed their pace for me. But I'm recovering fast.

Let's play I-spy, Pete announces.

You start, Glenda sings.

It's like walking with a group of children. I cast about for some likely object to spy. Crows pecking in the rough grass? A bank of alpine roses? What if you don't get it soon enough and it's no longer visible?

Has to be visible for two hundred yards, Pete decides.

That's only about two minutes, Glenda objects.

Okay, five hundred yards. And we each have a max of ten questions, closed questions.

Right then. I spy with my little eye something beginning with P.

You didn't put your fingers round your eye, Glenda objects.

You have to make a monocle!

I remove my sunglasses, bend finger and thumb round my right eye, and repeat, Something beginning with P.

Clue! Obligatory clue! Pete demands.

When do the five hundred yards begin? I ask.

Pete! Glenda cries and does a little skip and a jump. P for Pete! Yes?

Strictly speaking, Pete isn't a something, is he? So, no.

A guess counts as two questions, Pete warns.

Damn!

And the five hundred yards start after the obligatory clue.

I think for a moment. Okay. In case. That's the clue.

In case?

There's some discussion as to whether this is a legitim-
ate clue. Shouldn't it be something to do with size, material, distance?

I'm sticking with it, I tell them. And the five hundred
yards has begun.

In case of landslides? Pete asks.

No.

Is it near or far? Glenda asks.

Didn't we say only closed questions?

Okay, is it near?

Define near?

Less than ten yards.

Fewer! Pete cries.

Yes and no, I answer.

Yes and no?

Ah! So, is there more than one? Pete asks.

Pole! Glenda yells. Poles in case of snow. To mark the
road. I got it. I got it. I'm so damn good! She punches
the air.

You broke the rules, Pete objects. First Dan has to
answer my question and if he answers yes I have the right
to guess before the next player has their turn. You only got
it because of my smart question.

They argue over this for a couple of minutes and decide
to apply the rule in the future but to let this round stand.
One point to Glenda. I'm amazed. Was I in competition
with Margaret and Julia the same way? Was it just hidden
because we never played I-spy? Or sublimated in me telling stories of my various humiliations?

The landscape is a puzzle of greens and greys now.

Grasses and ferns and dark heathers. No trees. To the west, beyond the deep Ticino valley, the sky is white with cloud. Despite the altitude, the air has grown sultry.

I spy with my little eye – Glenda makes her monocle and turns it right and left, up and down, so as to give nothing away – something beginning with H. And my obligatory clue is 'melancholy'.

Subjective! What's melancholy for you might be cheerful for me.

I don't think so, Glenda says.

There's a moment's silence while we look around. But only a moment.

Hut, Pete cries. Hut!

Glenda rolls her eyes. Damn!

In one! Hole in fucking one! There must be an extra point for that.

Up ahead, to the left of the path, a small hut leans against the outcropping rock. The roof is a rusty corrugated iron. As we approach, it seems abandoned. The doors and windows are broken. Discarded machinery, an old toilet seat. But at the corner of the building there's a modern plastic wheelie bin. Apparently waiting for the refuse men.

Told you it was melancholy, Glenda sighs.

The game goes on. Except we can't guess Pete's clues. His strategy is to select some generic element of a larger phenomenon. A blade of grass. A clod of earth. A wisp of cloud. It's cheating, Glenda decides. For a while they debate the rules back and forth. To the west the clouds are thickening, but we haven't lost the sun yet. A couple of hikers appear, coming the other way, clicking their pointed trekking poles on the asphalt. Wussies, Pete thinks. Impressive boots, Glenda says. At the end of the day, I wonder, will I think of myself as a winner or a loser? A good man or a bad? Was the affair with Julia victory or defeat? Virtue or vice? The alpine uplands stretch away in every direction, fluid, furrowed, vast. High above, a jet trail pushes south, soundless, utterly disconnected from the world below. Glenda is insisting on a new rule. For less advanced participants? Pete needles. My Julia years, I realise, were utterly disconnected from the rest of my life. On the other hand, it was the only time I was really alive. That is the truth. The only episode to redeem a grey ocean of waste.

Now comes a whistle. Listen! Pete stops. We stop and wait. When Glenda makes to speak, Pete lifts a finger to his lips. Sudden and shrill, it comes again. Down in the valley. A short, sharp whistle.

Marmot, Glenda whispers. She gets her phone out for a photo.

The whistle comes a third time, but we can't see the creature. The sound is piercing, but barely lasts a second.

Look up! Pete says.

Sure enough, in the blue above our heads a dark speck is circling. Even more discrete than the jet trail, but absolutely connected to the earth beneath. Where all the marmots are now hidden in their burrows.

Somewhere round here we turn, Pete announces. A track to our right leads to a long low prefab with half a dozen cars parked outside. But that's not what we're looking for. Our path leaves the road fifty yards further on, winding down beside the low building into a gulley that quickly narrows then drops out of sight. There's no view down into the Ticino valley, no sight of Airolo, just the impression of a wide deep chasm before the mass of mountains the other side, their peaks now hidden in storm clouds. I brace myself. We have to crouch under a line of barbed wire to get on to the path. Three or four men talking together outside the prefab must have seen us but make no comment.

We can't be trespassing if it's on the app, Pete says.

There are no signs here. No red-and-white flashes. For a while we seem to be following an old tractor track, which is encouraging. Made of whitish stones. But long in disuse. As the slope grows steeper, deep ruts appear. The surface has been washed away. I'm nursing my knee already. Then the track rounds a spur to the left and there's another abandoned hut. Same stone walls and iron roof. Dirt and droppings. Broken glass.

Melancholy, Glenda repeats.

Outside, a water trough is choked with weeds, then there are fifty flattish yards of lush green, a tiny field almost, with some kind of fodder crop run wild. Big dark floppy leaves. Here the track ends. And now there's that whistle again. There! Pete cries. Running into the hut!

Glenda and I missed it. She goes to investigate, but comes back shaking her head. Something stinks in there. We stand and look around. The place feels eerie: the empty hut, the ruined track, last year's crops run to seed. For some reason I think of Gerhard. From the west comes a distant rumble. The sun has fallen behind the clouds.

Let's move, Pete says.

But where is the path? We cross the spinach field – it looks like spinach – and cast about. A trickle of a stream is flowing in from our left. In a deep crevasse. Oh, for a pink woman, Glenda sighs.

Further down, Pete picks up the path again. We zigzag after him, ankles angled against the steep slope. You can just make out a thread of trail; the grass is thinner and there are patches of dry mud. But no footprints. No one has passed this way in a while. The grass is a yellowish green, lank and coarse, lying flat against the earth which is steeper with every step. There are frequent stops while Pete consults his app. Fucking location blob. He stares from phone to landscape and back, trying to establish where the path must be. We seem to be funnelling down into a kind of ravine, which then opens and drops into the Ticino valley. The rocky masses disturb the GPS. The blue blob won't stay still. A couple of hundred yards ahead the land disappears, as if we were about to be shot off the mountain in a waterfall. Three thousand feet, I remember.

We should be moving away from the stream, Pete thinks. Out of the ravine. He works round the side of the slope to the right where the incline is not so steep. Glenda follows. I'm hopping behind. What would our life together have been like in the end? I wonder. It was unimaginable and always was. Now the path reappears for a couple of minutes. But plunging downward. As if you were trying to walk from top to bottom of a sphere. Then it's gone altogether. I catch up with the other two; the slope is so steep Glenda is leaning against the mountainside. The grass is a tufty, uneven carpet. There are no bushes or trees. No outcropping rock. Nothing to hang on to. You have to point your feet.

Wait, Pete says. Phone in hand he tracks back a few yards, follows a suspicion of a path downward, disappears, then reappears to the right, skirting the slope, some way below.

Found it!

I have to get down on my backside, arms outspread. My legs are trembling. There are about twenty yards of relatively easy scrambling, then nothing. Across the valley, lightning flickers. The late afternoon is hushed and still.

Houston, Pete says. We have a problem.

Maybe go back to the road, I suggest.

And then what?

Back to the Gotthard. Down the main trail.

Take for ever, Glenda objects.

Defeat, Pete sighs.

There's a constant dance of lightning now. Over to the west. And a long low rumbling, a great steel ball rolling down the valley.

Airolo is directly below, Pete says. Or almost. Get down here and we'll be in the shower by seven. Legs under the table by seven thirty.

It's a nice thought. Everyone is quiet for a moment.

Look, I tell them, we don't have to stay together. You two go on. I'll just be a burden. Let me turn back.

No way, Glenda says. We're in this together. You turn back we turn back.

Rain. Pete holds out a hand. The first fat drops splash into the stillness.

Fact is, I'm still capable of climbing back up now. But maybe not if we go further.

I sense they are struggling. They were ready for complications on the higher peaks, but not on a grassy slope where their professional app showed a path. On the other hand I feel extremely lucid. I just want to get off this mountain safely. Perhaps there's a bus to Airolo from the Gotthard. My walk is over. This whole story is over.

We've got to decide, Glenda says. Her voice has a new sharpness.

Pete frowns. Give me ten minutes to explore a bit further. If it doesn't look good, we go back. Okay?

He doesn't want to have been wrong about this path. There's a tension between them.

Do you have a signal? Glenda asks.

Pete has two bars. I have one. With my battery at 5 per cent. Glenda has none. Pete and I exchange numbers.

I reckon this is good for about half an hour.

More than enough, he says. I'll be quick. He consults his map again and studies the lie of the land. It should be over there, he points, and sets off diagonally down to the right. He's surprisingly nimble for a man of his size, walking with one hand on the mountainside, ready to fall against it if need be. Wey-hey and up she rises! he sings. For a while we can see his red cap tracking back and forth precipitously below. Then he's gone behind a spur.

Glenda sits on her haunches. Fuck, she says.

A gust of wind brings some real rain. I pull off my pack and get out my waterproof.

Fuckin' app, she says. Stupid map's not up to date. Then they charge you for the things as well.

Even standing still I have the impression I'm about to slide down the slope.

Pete is pretty experienced, though, right?

Not really. She sighs. He gets these enthusiasms. Kayaking. Canyoning. They don't last.

But I don't want to hear her speak badly of him.

Maybe put on your waterproof?

Right, she says. She seems troubled.

With the rain the temperature is tumbling. You can see a squall moving down the mountainside across the valley. A grey blur. On the horizon above, the cloud is brighter, as if the sun might still pierce through. The scene is spectacular in its depth, the abyss where the land falls away beneath us, the high crags opposite, half in the cloud, the lightning flickering against the greyness.

Stupid stupid stupid, getting ourselves in the shit down here, Glenda mutters. We read up everything on the Pizzo. Watched videos. We were super prepared. And nothing about this place. I don't think we even checked how close the contour lines were on the map.

Like finding yourself on a roof with no way down.

Too true. She pulls a blue hood over her hair. Want a mint?

We suck and wait. It feels like the ten minutes are almost up. Glenda gets to her feet and peers down through the rain. She shakes her head.

Grass will be getting slippy, I reflect.

You bet. Damn. This is a no-brainer. We'll have to climb up and go back to the pass. Phone Pete and let's get moving. I'm getting cold.

Are you sure? Give him another minute?

Suddenly I feel the pathos of Pete's situation. I want the boy to be proved right. The path picks up a few yards down. He's followed it a way and it gets better and better. The treacherous grass ends. There are woods. Trees to break a fall.

Call him, Glenda says.

I press the green button and hand her the phone. She slips it under her hood out of the rain. Stands and waits. Come on, come on! I can just hear the faint ring tones through the patter of the rain. Don't tell me he hasn't got the fucking volume on, for Christ's sake.

I try to remember if I've heard Pete's phone ring during the day.

Wow!

Across the valley lightning splits the sky from top to bottom. A marmot whistles, twice. Then the thunder.

Glenda laughs. All we need is to be struck by fucking lightning. Pete! she yells down into the void. Pete, get your dumb arse up here and let's get moving.

The rain is falling steadily. We're completely exposed on this empty slope.

Maybe we should move back a way. Find a flatter place at least.

Not until Pete comes. How long's he been exactly?

I'm not sure. Twenty minutes?

We call again. Again the phone rings and rings. Finally an answering service clicks in. My battery is down to 3 per cent. Suddenly the rain is torrential, driven by a blast of wind. We turn our backs to it and crouch in the grass.

Earth smells good, Glenda chuckles.

Water starts to stream down the slope all round us. I'm cold and stiff.

Pete! Glenda yells. Fucking hell. She's crouched with her face to the ground, strands of hair falling from her hood. Why in God's name doesn't he answer?

After a moment, she says, Dan, I'm sorry, we've really fucked up big time, here. What a pair of losers.

We'll be fine, I tell her. But almost at once it occurs to me, We should call the emergency services. What do you think?

Glenda seems astonished by the idea. He'll be back any minute, she says.

Do you know what the number is? I ask.

No. Get on the net and find it. And I'll go down and fetch the idiot.

We're on our haunches side by side, rain clattering on our capes, fingers digging into the grass.

It would be mad to try and get down there in this, I tell her.

I'm fucking furious, she says. He's so stupid. So frustrated with his job he has to play Mr Mountain Guide. He knows nothing about the mountains. Fucking nothing!

Do I call the emergency services or not?

Find the number.

Sheltering the phone under my chest I open Chrome,

type in Switzerland emergency . . . There's an invitation to complete the search with 'number'. I go for it.

112.

The rain eases. As if a tap had been turned. The wind drops. Glenda jumps to her feet. I've got to go and see, damn it. Maybe he's hurt himself.

Before I can object she is clambering down the slope. She keeps her face to the ground, as if she were climbing down a ladder, kicking her toes into the grass, hands grabbing at tufts. Fuck fuck fuck, she's cursing. She stands up to get a view of where Pete went, turns to move sideways across the slope and slips.

Glenda!

It's so fast. She twists, falls, rolls over, thumping the ground, arms and legs flailing to grip. From where I'm standing it seems she must go over the edge of the world. But the fall slows. She's got hold of something for a second. Or dug a boot in. She clutches and kicks. Finally she's lying still, below me to the right, her red cape ridden up her back, pack askew, legs spread wide.

Fuck, the voice comes clearly, almost calmly.

Are you okay? Can you hold on?

Ankle is killing me. And my knee. There's a short silence. I'm fucking terrified.

But can you hold on?

I don't know. Fuck.

I take off my pack and have to press it into the grass so it doesn't roll down. What do I have with me? Nothing. No rope, no crampons, or hammer, or pitons.

I don't think I can hold on here, she wails. I think I'm going to fall. Jesus.

I have my penknife. Teacher's Boy Scout pocketknife, Julia mocked. I pull off my cape to free my arms, then leaning sideways against the slope, with my right knee dug in and my left foot stretched down, feeling for some tuft that might offer a little purchase, I slash at the grass and try to dig the blade in. The soil is hard and shallow and stony.

Just hang on. I'm going to cut footholds down to you. Don't do anything.

Actually it's handholds I'm digging. Shallow little holes where I can put my fingers. Muddy holes. The slope is soaking. But they don't have to hold my weight. Just stop me slipping. Glenda is moaning and cursing below me.

Keep still. Hang on.

What a prat I am, what a prat, what a prat.

At the fourth or fifth excavation, I hear my phone's death rattle. For some reason this raises a smile. Finally my left foot is almost beside her right hand.

I'm going to kick out a handhold just above you, okay. For Christ's sake don't try to stand or anything. Stay pressed on the grass.

I feel so heavy.

How much does your pack weigh?

Twenty pounds. Ish.

If you can slip it off easily, dump it. Let it go.

I'd have to get my cape off.

Forget it.

Fucking ankle's awful. I feel sick.

Grin and bear.

I'm going to faint.

Bite your lip.

I kick and kick and kick and kick until finally the surface gives, then climb a step away.

Can you reach?

There's a brief wait. I have my face to the grass and can't look.

Yes. Got it.

Great.

I've no idea how long it all takes. I'm utterly soaked. Breathing hard. Nails broken in the stony earth. Clothes filthy. But after interminable grunts and screams and just one frightening slither, we're both back where I left my pack. Glenda can't stand on her left ankle. She's bruised and bedraggled. She sits and sobs. But suddenly stops.

Pete must have fallen. We have to get help.

The thunder hasn't let up, the rain is coming down in sheets again.

Okay, so, we climb back towards the road and as soon as your phone has a signal, we call the emergency services.

She can't walk. I have to give her a shoulder to lean on and we inch sideways across the slope, backs to the mountain, face to the void, pointing our feet at each step.

I can't believe we don't have trekking poles, she says. Always took the piss out of wimps with trekking poles. I can't believe I let him go ahead in a place like that, with the rain and everything. So stupid. You think you're smart and instead you're so fucking stupid. Maybe he's broken his neck, he's lying there dying. I can't believe I stopped you from calling for help when—

Shut up, Glenda! Concentrate. You can think about it afterwards. Maybe twenty years afterwards, the thought goes through my mind.

She stops. You should go on without me. Take the phone. I'm too slow.

First we get you to a safe place. Then I'll go.

The rain is ploughing furrows in the slope now. It seems the whole mountain is sliding towards us. An endless trickling and gurgling. Our feet are covered in slime.

Please, go now.

No.

I'm okay, she insists.

You're not okay. You're hysterical. And you have a broken ankle.

The lightning flickers. Hop by slow hop we shuffle back to the spinach field. At last it's flat enough to sit safely.

If you like we can get you to the hut.

Iron roof? In a thunderstorm?

You're right.

She pulls out her phone. Attached by a toggle to her belt. It seems to have survived the accident intact. In a red plastic case. There's plenty of battery.

Check the pattern lock.

Holding the screen under her cape, she shows me the pattern.

You do it.

We're huddled together. I can smell her warmth. The pattern is a simple zigzag.

Got it. Nothing else tricky?

No.

Do you remember where you last had a signal?

I definitely had one at the lake.

That's a long way.

I give her my pack to keep. I'll be quicker. There's an apple in there somewhere. Eat it.

For a moment we look each other in the eyes. Close up. She has a young round chubby face. Hair plastered to pink cheeks. Dark eyes. Crying.

Please don't let him be dead.

I'll be quick.

The storm has drifted across the valley. The evening sky flickers and cracks. I have no idea what time it is but climbing past the old hut then up the hairpins of the ruined track, I realise I feel good. I'm full of adrenalin. Doing what I have to do. Alive in the heavy rain. Not even cold, or not feeling it. Not worried about my knee or soaking feet, or my wet shorts rubbing at the groin. Little waves of mud and stones ripple down towards me. The caw of a crow somewhere. I feel strong. I stop to check the phone, sheltering it under my jacket. No signal. The screen shows a selfie of Glenda and Pete triumphant on a mountain top. I need to hurry.

On the last steep climb to the road, I see headlights. They're coming down in the direction of the pass. Sweeping through the rain. I try to run a few steps. It's hopeless. They're gone. But there is the big prefab where the path joins the road. I'd forgotten it. I slip under the barbed wire. If there were someone in the building now.

It's a minute's walk. The evening light is coming and going with the passing squalls. Bright and dark. The high moorland is glum. Running water everywhere. ALPE DI SORESCIA says a sign. FORMAGGI. A few yards along the access road there's a wire mesh gate. No cars parked in there now, but a tractor tucked against the wall of a low white building. Rain sparkles in the neon over the door. I look for a bell to ring. There isn't one. Anyone in? I yell. Hello! Hello there! *Attenzione!*

Two dogs explode from behind the building. German shepherds. They run straight at the fence and leap up against it, barking furiously. Flashing teeth and black fur in the teeming rain. I stumble back. Could their barking bring someone? I stand at a distance, watching the dogs get madder and madder as they try to lunge at me. What if there's a hole in the fence? Does it make sense to wait?

The road is easy. Only slightly downhill, unfolding through rugged outcrops into an immense twilight of rock and cloud and lightning. I can make good speed. I'm feeling strangely happy and at the same time very anxious for Pete. Jüngling Ludwig, I remember. A car surprises me. Why didn't I hear it? The first I know is the sharp honk of a horn. I jump aside, shouting, waving my arms, running after. It's gone.

I turn back to see if any more lights are coming. And check the phone again. Is it possible she turned the connectivity off? To save battery. I try to check, but this phone doesn't seem to work like mine. I manage to remove the pattern lock but can't find settings or Wi-Fi or airplane mode. Perhaps it will make an emergency call anyway. I

195

open the phone app and try 112. You have no service at the present moment.

I start to jog. Gingerly. So grateful it's not me lying at the bottom of a gulley. My knee sends a warning jab. The rain's eased and I'm keeping the phone in my hand now. Opening and closing the case to check. Now come a series of hairpins, down towards the dam. I can see a light at the bottom. Opening the phone, I find it's ringing. Silently.

I'm astonished. The sound must be off. Four white letters pulse in the centre of the screen. Pete. But I can't open the call. The screen won't respond to my fingers. Am I doing something wrong? Little red lines radiate from the name as it pulses, as though in a cartoon. Life is too ridiculous. I'm standing in the rain on a hairpin bend beside a snow-marker pole screaming with frustration. Nothing I do opens the call. As soon as the pulsing stops and Missed Call comes up I select that and press on Pete. Silence. Then a ring. The English ring tone. He answers at once.

Glenda.

It's Dan.

I can hear him breathing.

Are you okay?

There's a deep sigh. Pass me Glenda.

Glenda's hurt her ankle. I'm back up on the road. About to call the emergency services.

Again there's a pause.

I just called them.

112?

Yes.

And?

196

Another pause.

They're coming.

They know where you are?

Yes.

I'll call them for Glenda.

It's ok. I said there were others, further up. They know. I wanted to tell you not to try to come down.

Are you really okay?

He sighs.

You fell.

I was out, for a while. Let's end the call. In case the rescue people want me.

Putting the phone back in my pocket I realise, I need a pee. My mission is over, I can relax, take care of myself. At the side of the road I add my trickle to the water running down a rock, and notice something dark there. To my left. A few rags of dark fur. Maybe a marmot. Maybe a dog. It looks like the birds have had a feast.

I turn and climb back up the hairpins. This time I can enjoy the strangeness of the walk, the evening light bleeding out of the high moorland, the peaks turned silhouettes, the cool moist air, last spots of rain on my cheeks. The road seems longer now. Glenda will be in an agony of worry. But I don't speed up. I don't think I can. At the cheese factory the dogs must be asleep again. Everything is still. I lift the barbed wire beside the road and slither under. Nurse my knee down the sludge and stones of the track.

Glenda! I start to call from the hut. Through the spinach field. Glenda! Pete's okay.

Thank God!

She's dragged herself to a rock a little way up the slope off the path. Propped herself up there, on a ground sheet, wrapped in a space blanket.

He didn't say how badly he was hurt?

No. Your ankle?

Swollen. It's a football.

I've got some Ibuprofen.

Already took some.

Well done.

So this is how our long day ends, I think. Or pauses. We sit quietly, backs to the rock. Trusting someone will come. I pull a sweater out of my pack. I'm shivering. It's soaked. I must have left the thing open. She unwraps the space blanket. Come in beside? I pull the thin stuff round me. Foil-wrapped, huh?

Right. Speaking of which, I've got some chocolate somewhere. Want some?

Why not?

The last light has gone. The rain has stopped. A breeze is coming up. They'd better hurry, she says, munching her chocolate. Do you think they'll use a helicopter?

I've no idea. Whatever's fastest. From where they are.

Right.

I can't believe Pete is down there. In trouble. He wouldn't have called if he wasn't hurt.

Maybe just trapped. Unable to go on, unable to climb back.

Could be.

She takes my hand under the blanket. You're freezing.

I'm warming up.

It's very odd to be sitting shoulder to shoulder, hand in hand, with a woman I only really met this morning. Under a starry sky. We're exhausted. Somewhere behind us a pair of birds are twittering. The ground around is alive with the sound of water. The minutes pass.

I was wondering, she says, while you were away, why you had that crying fit, up on the mountain.

Oh. Old stuff.

You mind me asking?

Not really.

So?

Somewhere in the distance a dog is barking. Perhaps at the cheese factory.

I'm just curious, she says. You don't look the kind who would burst out crying. I thought you were a bit of a cold fish.

Well thanks.

You're welcome.

There's a long silence. I'm struck by a sudden awareness that the mountain is always here. Always. Day and night. These rocks and grasses. Peaks and crannies. Here the day Catherine died. The day General Suvorov captured the Devil's Bridge. Here tomorrow, should I decide to come back. Or in ten years. Or thirty when I will be dead.

So?

You really want to know?

To pass the time. To stop worrying about Pete.

Okay. So. Years ago I ran away with a married woman after a long affair. We came on a hike. To Switzerland. Then she heard her daughter had died, maybe an accident, maybe not. She hurried home. We never spoke to each other again.

No way, Glenda says.

We sit peering through the shadows, perhaps listening for the throb of a motor.

And did you climb the Pizzo Centrale?

No. We didn't make it this far.

But that's why you came back to Switzerland? To revisit places.

I heard she had died and I wanted to see how I felt about it. After so long.

Interesting. And what do you feel?

I don't know. Sometimes nothing. Sometimes heartbroken. Sometimes happy.

She's quiet for a moment. I remember she works with disturbed children. It feels easy talking to her, sitting together in the damp mountain evening. Warming up a little now.

I feel, this happened, you know. That's what my life is. Part of it. I'm glad to be alive. I'm glad I came along with you two today, for example.

That's kind of you. Despite the cock-up.

Maybe because of it. In a way.

Getting me out of that hole.

It was a good moment when we were back on the path.

You bet. She sighs. Do you think I should marry Pete?

Ha! You're asking me? Like that.

Why not?

Social worker asks geography teacher.

Oh please. We're people. You seem very . . . grown up.

A grown-up cold fish!

If you like.

Has he proposed?

Hinted. I don't think he's sure either.

Do you want to?

Half. Half I'm afraid it's not the right thing.

I think about this. It's familiar territory.

Maybe there are no right things, just things you make right, or not, over time.

Deep!

I suppose one test is, can you really imagine marrying him?

But all at once there are voices. Above us. Dogs barking. A flicker of torchlight somewhere beyond the hut. We struggle to our feet, shouting and waving.

'I have availability'

In the toilets at Casualty, I pull my dry bag out of my pack. It contains one spare underwear, one pair of socks, one long-sleeved T-shirt, jeans. At least I'll be dry. We were forty minutes in the van. Our driver mainly silent. No doubt because neither of us speak Italian. That path, it is a trap, she offered at one point. We are bringing the body bags, you know, when we come here. Together this woman and I had helped Glenda hop back to the road. Arms linked behind her back. The other four, three men and a woman, went on down the slope for Pete. Both helicopters were out, they said, for an avalanche on the glacier. They knew exactly where he would be. They had ropes, crampons, stakes to hammer into the ground. A stretcher. They would carry him down to the valley floor.

Everything was done very fast. Our driver drove very fast, racing down the hairpins below the pass. I began to feel nauseous. Do you want to get off at Airolo? Glenda asked. She remembered I had booked a hotel. I'll keep you company, I said. Suddenly it occurred to her she could call Pete. Don't, I told her. They'll be with him now. They'll be busy. Now I go back to work, our driver said, turning into the hospital gate. For the first time, she smiled. She worked in a restaurant. In Lavorgo. She hadn't expected to be called out this evening. *Buona fortuna.*

Towards midnight Glenda is helped onto a wheelchair and taken for an examination. There is no news of Pete. He hasn't been brought here. We're in a place called Faido, but it seems the main hospital is in Bellinzona. Further south. There's a mill of sufferers in the waiting room. A crying child. A man with blood on his face. One neon tube is flickering. Sour smells. It's strange, I reflect, how accidents always happen to others, not me. I didn't get my fingers caught in the shredding machine. Was never in a car crash. Never fell into a wild river. I'm the one who waits for news, pays the taxi and buys the airline tickets, makes his shoulder available. It drove me crazy that she wouldn't cry on it. The only time this cold fish lost his cool. Had she already decided? I've often wondered. At the airport. On the plane. Was there something she knew but had never told me? Sometimes I suspected it was she had called her husband from the Albis Café that morning, not vice versa.

If only we had turned back, Glenda wails. They have taken X-rays, given her a crutch, and a sort of white nightshirt. She flops onto the seat beside me. In my head I keep replaying that moment when you said, Let's go back. I keep willing myself to say yes, to have said yes, then we'd all be fine, we'd be tucked up in bed. She slumps with her chin on her chest, shaking her head from side to side. Where the fuck is Pete? She tries to call, but his phone isn't answering. Maybe he sent a message to your phone, she says. There's a socket in the corner. No one will mind if you charge up.

Why would he send a message to me?

A nurse appears to take her away again. Signorina Glenda, she calls.

What state is Pete in? I wonder. A patient is pushed through the room on a trolley, groaning, his face swollen and bruised. I remember myself going back and back over the past, looking for the moment when a different decision might have led to a happy outcome. It's curious how possible that seems sometimes: to go back and do differently. You feel you really could. Times when I'd begged, Let's do it now, and she said, No, wait. Perhaps I should learn to be more assertive. I could have said, Kids, this path is a death trap, I'm turning back. Then actually turned and started walking. They would have followed. I can see them. They would have resented me, but who cares? Julia would have resented me if I had told the world about us, told her husband we were in love. You must let your wife go, Lawrence wrote. But it's crazy comparing such utterly different situations, so many years apart, at one thirty a.m. in the casualty ward of a small hospital in the Alps. A man vomiting on the row of seats opposite. His wife helping him to the bathroom. I rummage in my pack. An orderly arrives with a mop. Lawrence's pages are sodden. I have to peel them apart. He crossed the Gotthard with a seventeen-year-old Swiss boy he met on the path above Hospental. Was clearly drawn to the lad. To his youth and boldness. Describes pale cheeks and freckles. But then I'm drawn to Pete and Glenda. Lively young people.

Something frantic about them. When they arrived at Airolo the boy took the train back through the tunnel to Göschenen. To his family. Airolo is where the autobahn comes out from under the mountains, after ten miles of darkness. And the railway. Cars and carriages bursting out into southern sunshine. *The remembrance of the Ticino valley is a sort of nightmare to me*, Lawrence says. Julia's underlining is blurred on the damp paper. Remembrance is not a word one uses often. To do with death. Margaret's ashes in the Chapel of Remembrance. In York. Her hometown. I don't know where Julia is buried. Or Catherine. I didn't ask. I never visit the Chapel of Remembrance. Walking down to Bellinzona, Lawrence does nothing but complain about the roads and the railways and the industries. *As if we had created a steel framework, and the whole body of society were crumbling and rotting in between.* This is the person we decided to follow for our honeymoon! I stand up, walk over to the bin beside the hot drinks dispenser, squeeze the soaking pages into a pulp, and dump them.

Glenda comes back, on a wheelchair again. They have bandaged her ankle.

Tomorrow they'll put it in plaster. Seems it's a clean break.

That's good.

They're giving me a bed, she says. I asked about you, but they say they can't.

As we're speaking, Pete calls. Glenda turns her body to the wall. As if to be alone with him. Urgency, anxiety, tenderness pulse from her hunched shoulders as she listens. Closing the call she is in tears. He's broken something in his back. He fell and bounced a long way. Tomorrow they'll operate. Now she sobs. The tears flow and flow. Her body shakes. She opens her arms upwards towards me. I kneel and let her press her face into my chest. You need sleep, I tell her.

She recovers a little. What will you do?

I'll see. Maybe I'll just doze here, in the waiting room.

Your hotel?

Last check-in was at ten. It's miles back.

But . . .

Go to bed. Sleep.

Coffee from the machine is only 50 cents. I'm on my third. And another pack of chocolate wafers. It's pushing three a.m. No one has come in for a while. The neon above me flickers, striving and failing to turn itself on. The room is emptier now. A young couple are speaking in low voices. The woman is pregnant. An obese man has stretched himself out across four chairs.

Occasionally a door opens, a nurse calls. I've moved to a corner seat, beside the power socket. I turn on my phone and check the mail. Rachel wonders will I be passing through London on my return. She has something to ask me. I open Booking.com and write a line of apology to the hotel for not showing up. There was an accident. I'm in hospital, but okay. Why do I do this when they have taken my money already, when my absence has actually saved them time and effort? Presumably I want to suppose a relation of mutual concern, mutual respect, beyond the mechanical money principle. I don't like to leave people in the dark. As I was once left utterly in the dark. A notification tells me I still haven't replied to Frau Schönauer (Heike) who wrote to me six days ago. I remember the German woman's kindness, bringing me dinner and breakfast. She had freckles too, beneath short-sighted eyes. Being left in the dark is like falling, I realise. Falling falling falling. Are you sure, I tap in the message box, that it's my umbrella?

For a while I study Google Maps. I could follow Lawrence down to Italy. The lakes. The historic cities. But I've binned Lawrence. I'm not interested in Italy. Is it time to go home then? Time for the future? Faido has a station, I see. Twenty minutes' walk away. A first train leaves at 6.20. For Basel, of all places. But Grubenhof interests me even less than Italy. I don't want to see the beam where Gerhard hung himself. Of course, one could change at Zürich for Zürich Airport. Be there at 9.12. Really? Do I really want to be in Zürich Airport buying an expensive flight to London after a long sleepless night and another aborted mission? What is the future, I wonder, for a retired geography teacher? Who has lost his bearings. Online dating?

I try to make myself comfortable on my seat. Try to sleep. Should I feel obliged to stay on here, for Glenda and Pete? They have no need for me. Glenda's a competent young woman. Pete's in good hands. My head nods and jerks upright. They can sort things out themselves. I manage to wedge my pack between chair and wall to make a kind of pillow. Feeling oddly positive. Happy with the warmth of my breath and the comfort of my closed eyes. Stratigraphic sections, I tell Year 9, have many uses. Earthquake prediction, for example. Mineral exploration.

Am I dreaming? It feels like I'm still awake, still snuggling my head against my pack. But I can hear my classroom voice. I can see the children bent over their exercise books. In the flickering neon of the Casualty ward waiting room. Is it the coffee? Now I'm showing a slide. On the big screen in Room 5D. Igneous rocks pushing through a sedimentary crust. Sir! Sir! There's someone in the map! A figure is walking across the dikes and sills. Of the stratigraphic section. Which is silly because this is a slide projector. But the whole situation is silly, teaching Year 9 with my head lolling on the backpack I bought years ago to make my escape with Julia. Thank God I brought my pocketknife. The man is walking from left to right. Across a mudstone scarp. Constantly looking over his shoulder. Is he Cretaceous, sir? cries someone in the back row. Is he Jurassic? The class is getting rowdy. I'm losing control. He's looking for somewhere to pee, sir! Hope he doesn't fall off the cliff. Assert your authority. Kids, this man is looking for the source of the river, can't you see? I use my pointer to indicate the river. It's the Reuss. I'm climbing a steep slope where water bubbles from every mossy crevasse. On all sides. But which one is the source? The real source? I'm ankle deep, knee deep. I'm swimming in a place where many waters meet. In a wide swirling whirlpool. Far out to sea. Four or five figures turning in the strong current. White bodies. All women. We'll have to swim hard to get out of here, girls, I shout. These people need help. Swim, swim! But they seem happy to be turning and turning in the grey water. In flickering light. My freestyle is getting me nowhere. The water is warm. Relax, I tell myself. You are marooned in a dream. That's all. A waking dream. In the Casualty ward waiting room. I can hear women's voices. Doors banging. Long hair floating on the water. Perhaps they've brought someone in from the mountains. From the glacier. Someone who's fallen. I'm falling through the bottom of the whirlpool. This is the way out. How wonderful dreams are. All colours and feelings. There's a loud thump. A group of people are gathered round something on the ground. What is it? I land lightly beside them and bend down to look. There's animal fur. There's blood. But this is Julia's dream! I raise my eyes and gaze into hers.

The doors of the waiting room have been wedged open and three stretchers wheeled in. Bodies strapped down. Two men in orange jackets are filling in forms at Reception. My watch tells me it's four thirty. A drama is unfolding. I saw her face again. It's gone now. Closing my eyes, I go over the last moments of the dream. The fall. The strangely soft landing. As if I were a bird. The crowd of people round the animal's body. Look up and find her eyes. They really were hers. I can't bring them back. But I remember she was smiling. Blankly. Like the blank smiling faces in the meditation website. Was she aware she was looking at me? I go back over the dream searching for details. The maps on the classroom wall. Of the five continents. Women's arms flung outward on the water. As I fell it was dark, but not a nightmare. I wasn't afraid. The people in the crowd were wearing overcoats, at a bus stop. The animal was black or grey. A dog. Every single animal, it occurs to me, sooner or later, has to ask of the world a place to leave its bones. The cheerful Mr Burrow, Julia laughs. It's curious how lucid I feel, in this waiting room where urgent voices are calling. In Italian. In German. A bell is ringing. Curious that I'm allowed to stay here, quite uninvolved, while life and death unfolds around me. You wonder sometimes if the dead don't die in our place. They really were her eyes and they did know they were smiling into mine. Beckoning? For the first time I wonder if it was the meditation retreat that ended our love. As much as Catherine's death. Julia bought into something there that made our relationship meaningless. Fear of the arising of mind and matter? I hadn't thought of this before. She underwent some kind of conversion. *Intimations of Buddhism in D. H. Lawrence*. But it hardly matters. The thoughts come and go, and the dreams and anxieties, and the voices in the Casualty ward with the whine of the coffee machine and a distant bell. Pretty pointless of Lawrence, I reflect, to keep trying to distinguish between real and unreal. And now there is a loud ding on my phone. I should have turned off the volume. Notification from Booking.com. You have a new message.

Naturally I am sure it is yours, Herr Burrow. If you tell me an address, I will send it you. Frau Schönauer (Heike).

I shake my head and sit upright. Somewhere outside a man is shouting. Two of the trolleys have gone. At five fifteen a woman sends me a message about a non-existent umbrella. How crazy is that? I'm always up early, she said that morning. Bringing me coffee and cake. Suddenly I feel cold, sitting in the Casualty ward waiting room, in my jeans and T-shirt. The doors are still wedged open. Orange jackets hurrying in and out. Both helicopters out for an avalanche. A woman with a toddler in her arms is crooning softly. I should have spread my sweater somewhere to dry.

Naturally I am sure it is yours.

Is it at all possible, I wonder, that I was wrong? That I did in fact pack my little windproof Samsonite? Companion of so many rainy walks to school. I suppose I could ask her if it's grey. On the other hand, if she's so sure . . .

Dear Frau Schönauer, I type, do you perhaps have a room available this evening? If so, I could spare you the effort of going to the post office.

I sort through my clothes, separating the muddy from the clean, wrapping my filthy knife in tissue. Now I'm on my feet. The pack feels heavier than it should. Perhaps with things being wet. Or me not having slept. But in myself I feel lighter. Much lighter. Outside, I find the hospital is actually in the country. Surrounded by fields. A long narrow modern building, walls opening outward from a narrow base, like the hull of a ship, left by receding floodwaters. A blackbird is singing. The grass is dewy. There's a sliver of moon. Almost at once you climb a bridge over the railway lines. The faint roar in the distance must be the autobahn. But the lane into the village is quiet. Gentle slopes and curves. Everything is easy and ordinary. The pavements clean and tidy. Houses and gardens well kept. A handsome old hotel dwarfs the tiny station. Hotel Bahnhof. A smell of baking bread.

It's five past six. Dawn is creeping down the slope across the valley. I decide to trust my luck and purchase a ticket to Jestetten. I'm getting used to these machines. I know their complications. Three hours and fifteen minutes. I can pay with my credit card. Changes at Arth and Zürich. There's a white stone bench on the platform. It's chilly. An older couple appear with coffee cups in their hands. Red backpacks. I close my eyes, to breathe and wait. Am I falling or flying? Just as the rails begin to tick in the early-morning hush, my phone vibrates and dings again.

Dear Herr Burrow, I have availability. How many days do you wish to stay?

Born in Manchester, **Tim Parks** grew up in London and studied at Cambridge and Harvard. He lives in Milan. He is the acclaimed author of novels, non-fiction and essays, including *Europa*, *A Season with Verona*, *Teach Us to Sit Still*, *Italian Ways* and *The Hero's Way: Walking with Garibaldi from Rome to Ravenna*. He has been shortlisted for the Booker Prize and has won many awards for both his work in English and his translations from the Italian, which include works by Alberto Moravia, Italo Calvino, Roberto Calasso, Antonio Tabucchi and Niccolò Machiavelli.